And Now You Know

Mind-Blowing Stories from History and Pop Culture

Cody Tucker

Copyright © 2025 Cody Tucker
All rights reserved.
ISBN- 979-8-218-66926-3

Dedication

To Mom and Dad—

Thank you for always being there for me and raising me to be the man I am today. I owe everything to you both and I appreciate you more than you know.

To my grandparents Johnny and Brenda McCollum—

Your encouragement and support have meant the world to me. Thank you both for fostering my curiosity and always lending an ear to my endless facts and stories.

To my high school teachers Ms. Roberts and Mr. Simmons—

I am forever thankful for the wisdom you've shared and the passion for learning you instilled in me. The gratitude I feel for the lessons you have taught me goes beyond words.

TABLE OF CONTENTS

PART 1: HISTORY
CHAPTER 1: WHACKJOBS AND WEIRDOS 1
CHAPTER 2: UNITED STATES HISTORY 18
CHAPTER 3: CRAZY COINCIDENCES 36
CHAPTER 4: BRUSHING SHOULDERS WITH THE NAZIS 51
CHAPTER 5: PRESIDENTS AND LEADERS 61
CHAPTER 6: WHERE DID THAT COME FROM? 74
CHAPTER 7: HISTORICAL TRUE CRIME 85
CHAPTER 8: SCIENCE GONE WRONG 101
CHAPTER 9: CLOSE CALLS AND STRANGE DEATHS 115
CHAPTER 10: ODDITIES 131

PART 2: POP CULTURE
CHAPTER 1: THE NOT-SO GOLDEN AGE OF HOLLYWOOD 145
CHAPTER 2: POP CULTURE CRIME SPREE 162
CHAPTER 3: INCREDIBLE ORIGIN STORIES 178
CHAPTER 4: STRANGE DEATHS 194
CHAPTER 5: SPORTS LEGENDS 206
CHAPTER 6: SEXS, DRUGS, AND ROCK N' ROLL 219
CHAPTER 7: BAD BEHAVIOR 235
CHAPTER 8: THE STORY BEHIND THE STORY 249
CHAPTER 9: HEORES AND HELLRAISERS 268
CHAPTER 10: HORROR AND THE PARANORMAL 282

Preface

History is overflowing with epic tales—famous figures, incredible ideas, and turning points that shaped the world. But just beneath the surface lies a goldmine of lesser-known stories: the bizarre, the overlooked, and the oddly fascinating. We all share a natural curiosity for these hidden corners of the past, especially the strange twists and the dark side of seemingly ordinary people and events. This book grew out of countless late-night rabbit holes, stacks of obscure reading, and the three most beautiful words in the English language: "Did you know…?"

I've always been fascinated by the lesser-known corners of the past: the bizarre events, the dark side of history and pop culture, unlikely coincidences, and characters who somehow slipped through the cracks of most textbooks. This collection of easily digestible stories brings together some of my favorite tales from history and pop culture that will hopefully leave you shocked, stunned, and ready for another one.

Some stories might surprise you. Others might make you rethink what you thought you knew. Whether you're a trivia addict, a history nerd, a pop culture junkie, or just someone who enjoys a good "Wait, what?!" moment, I hope you find something in these pages that surprises you, makes you laugh, or at least helps you impress your friends.

Thanks for joining me on this journey into the unknown and unexplored.

PART 1

HISTORY

CHAPTER 1

WHACKJOBS AND WEIRDS

THE ASSASSIN'S ASSASSIN

Thomas "Boston" Corbett was born on January 29, 1832, in London, England. At the age of eight, he immigrated to the United States with his family. As a young boy, Corbett worked as a milliner's apprentice, where daily exposure to mercury—unbeknownst to him—would later contribute to severe mental health issues.

Corbett's early years were marked by tragedy when his wife died, leaving him devastated. Seeking a fresh start, he moved to Boston but fell into chronic alcohol abuse. During a drinking binge, he encountered a Methodist preacher who helped him recover, sparking a profound religious transformation. By 1857, Corbett had become a fervent street preacher in Boston, known for his passionate and unconventional personality.

His devotion to his faith reached extreme levels. In 1858, after an encounter with two prostitutes, he interpreted a Bible passage literally and castrated himself with scissors to maintain celibacy. Despite this shocking act, he devoted himself to charity, assisting the homeless, alcoholics, and unemployed.

In 1861, Corbett enlisted in the Union Army, driven by his anti-slavery convictions. His military service was turbulent; he was court-martialed and discharged in 1863 but later re-enlisted.

In April 1865, his regiment participated in President Lincoln's funeral procession and was later assigned to capture John Wilkes Booth, the assassin.

Booth was cornered in a Virginia barn, which was set on fire to force him out. Through a crack in the barn, Corbett fired a fatal shot with his Colt revolver, claiming Booth had aimed a gun. Booth was dragged from the burning structure and died hours later.

After the war, Corbett returned to preaching and millinery work, but mercury exposure worsened his erratic behavior. In 1887, he was confined to the Topeka Asylum for the Insane after a violent outburst. On May 26, 1888, he escaped and vanished, never to be seen again.

THE GREEK FREEK

Diogenes was a Greek philosopher born in the late 400s BCE, renowned for his radical views on poverty, self-sufficiency, and his rejection of societal norms. A founder of the Cynic school of philosophy, he believed in living with nothing and famously chose to sleep in a large ceramic jar rather than a conventional home.

Diogenes was known for his provocative and unconventional behavior. He would stand outside brothels, begging for money while urging patrons to spend their wealth on charity instead of vice. Ironically, he often used the very money he collected to visit the brothels he publicly condemned.

His contempt for societal conventions extended to his behavior in public spaces. He was notorious for shocking the public by masturbating in the marketplace and defecating in temples, acts meant to challenge societal hypocrisy. Diogenes also openly mocked other philosophers, particularly Plato.

He would disrupt Plato's lectures by loudly eating or interrupting his discussions, ridiculing his ideas as overly abstract and disconnected from reality.

One of the most legendary encounters in Diogenes' life was with Alexander the Great. When Alexander expressed his admiration and offered to grant him any wish, Diogenes responded with utter indifference, saying, "Yes, stand out of my sunlight."

THE LIFE OF TIMOTHY DEXTER

Timothy Dexter, born in 1747 in Massachusetts, is remembered as one of history's most eccentric and unexpectedly successful businessmen. Despite being uneducated and often ridiculed as a fool, Dexter's remarkable ability to profit from bizarre ventures has left an indelible mark on history.

His neighbors, frustrated by his eccentricity and arrogance, tried to humiliate him with a prank. They convinced him to ship bedwarmers to the hot, humid West Indies, expecting financial ruin. To their astonishment, the bedwarmers sold quickly when local molasses producers repurposed them for industrial use. Dexter, instead of failing, made a tidy profit. Encouraged by this success, he followed another ill-conceived suggestion and shipped wool mittens to the West Indies. Once again, luck intervened—a Siberia-bound ship purchased all the mittens, earning Dexter yet another windfall.

With his newfound wealth, Dexter built a lavish mansion in Newburyport, Massachusetts, complete with statues of Napoleon Bonaparte, George Washington, and, naturally, himself. This display of vanity cemented his reputation as an odd and self-important figure.

Dexter's peculiar behavior extended to his personal life. At one party, he announced his wife had died, only for her to appear alive moments later. Dexter, refusing to admit the lie, claimed she was her own ghost. Most famously, he staged his own funeral to observe the attendees. While pleased with the turnout, he berated his wife for her visible grief, even appearing mid-funeral to scold her with a stick.

Timothy Dexter's life, a mix of absurdity and fortune, remains a testament to improbable success. His outlandish escapades have made him a uniquely unforgettable figure in American History.

FROM FRIENDS TO FOES

In the 1920s, Arthur Conan Doyle, the creator of Sherlock Holmes, became a passionate advocate of the spiritualist movement, which claimed to communicate with the dead through practices like seances. During this time, he developed a friendship with famed escape artist and magician Harry Houdini, who was grieving the loss of his mother, who had passed away in 1913.

Wanting to bring comfort to Houdini, Conan Doyle offered to conduct a seance with his daughter acting as the medium. The plan was for Houdini to speak to Conan Doyle's daughter, who would then convey his words to the spirit of his mother. She would then write down the spirit's responses and pass them back to Houdini.

However, Houdini immediately grew suspicious when all of the messages were written in flawless English—a language his Hungarian mother did not speak. His doubts deepened when the spirit made no mention of the fact that the day of the seance was his mother's birthday, a detail he felt she surely would have acknowledged. Feeling betrayed by what he saw as a cruel deception, Houdini became a vocal critic of spiritualism and made it his mission to expose fraudulent mediums. This included his former friend, Sir Arthur Conan Doyle, whom he publicly denounced and harbored resentment toward for the rest of his life.

THE EMPEROR WHO NEVER WAS

In 1859, a man named Joshua Norton declared himself "Emperor of the United States and Protector of Mexico" in San Francisco. Clad in a full imperial uniform, complete with epaulettes and a feathered hat, Norton patrolled the streets, inspecting sidewalks and construction sites. He meticulously documented his observations, submitting detailed reports to local newspapers and even the police. As self-proclaimed emperor, he issued a series of whimsical decrees, including one that dismissed the Governor of Virginia for hanging abolitionist John Brown and another that boldly dissolved the entire United States government.

Remarkably, the people of San Francisco embraced Norton's eccentricity, treating him with the respect and reverence befitting a true monarch. He printed his own currency, which local businesses accepted as legal tender, allowing him to eat and drink for free throughout the city. Norton's unique charm even caught the attention of a young Mark Twain, who lived in San Francisco during Norton's reign. Twain was so captivated by the self-proclaimed emperor that he later modeled the character of the King in The Adventures of Huckleberry Finn after him.

When Emperor Norton passed away in 1880, the city mourned the loss of its beloved and unconventional ruler. An estimated 10,000 people attended his funeral, paying tribute to the man who, despite his imaginary throne, had captured San Francisco's heart and become a symbol of individuality and eccentricity. Joshua Norton's legacy endures as a testament to the power of imagination and the city's enduring spirit of acceptance.

CULT OF PYTHAGORAS

Pythagoras, born around 570 BCE, is widely recognized for the Pythagorean theorem, but his life was marked by eccentricities and mysticism. Beyond his achievements in mathematics, he founded Pythagoreanism, a philosophical and religious movement that emphasized the mystical significance of numbers.

His followers adhered to rigid daily routines and strict dietary restrictions, including a peculiar ban on beans, as Pythagoras believed they harbored souls. By the age of 60, his movement had amassed over a thousand loyal disciples who revered him as a divine figure with supernatural abilities.

In 495 BCE, the Pythagorean meeting house was attacked and burned down. While many of his followers perished, Pythagoras and a handful of survivors managed to escape. However, his ultimate fate remains shrouded in mystery. Most historical accounts suggest that he and his remaining disciples eventually succumbed to starvation while in hiding, around the age of 75.

Despite his unconventional beliefs and mysterious demise, Pythagoras's contributions to mathematics have stood the test of time, solidifying his status as one of history's most influential yet enigmatic thinkers.

ROCKETS AND RITUALS

In 1939, Jack Parsons, the pioneering rocket scientist and founder of the Jet Propulsion Laboratory, became deeply influenced by the occult teachings of Aleister Crowley. While living in a bungalow in Pasadena, California, Parsons began hosting gatherings of fellow occult enthusiasts, where they conducted various rituals inspired by Crowley's philosophy.

One of the regular attendees at these gatherings was a young L. Ron Hubbard, who would later go on to establish Dianetics and found the Church of Scientology. Hubbard eventually moved into Parsons' home, becoming his close confidant and sidekick.

In December 1945, Parsons and Hubbard embarked on an ambitious occult ritual known as the Babalon Working, which aimed to summon the goddess Babalon into human form. As part of the ritual, Parsons performed a series of elaborate ceremonies, including masturbating on sacred stone tablets while Hubbard took detailed notes.

Shortly after the ritual, a young woman named Marjorie Cameron appeared at Parsons' home. Convinced that she was the earthly manifestation of the goddess they had summoned, Parsons began a romantic relationship with her as part of his practice of Sex Magick.

Meanwhile, his then-partner, Sara Northrup—who was also his ex-girlfriend's younger sister—became romantically involved with L. Ron Hubbard, leading to a bitter fallout between Parsons and his former friend.

Amid this turmoil, Parsons made plans to move to Mexico with Marjorie Cameron, intending to set up a laboratory to continue his rocketry experiments. However, on June 17, 1952, just one day before his planned departure, Parsons was working with explosives in his home laboratory when he accidentally dropped a can of fulminate of mercury. The resulting explosion was catastrophic, tearing off his right forearm and inflicting severe injuries to his face, legs, and remaining arm.

He was found alive but succumbed to his injuries shortly after being taken to the hospital, ending the extraordinary life of a man who bridged the worlds of science and the occult.

MOZART THE MANIAC

Mozart, hailed as one of the greatest composers in history, displayed extraordinary musical talent from an early age, composing his first pieces at just five years old. By his teenage years, he had already written half of the symphonies that would cement his legacy. Despite his undeniable genius, Mozart was also known for his eccentric and often crude sense of humor.

In one peculiar incident, he composed a piece for a woman with a generously endowed chest, deliberately arranging the music so that she would have to cross her arms repeatedly while playing the piano. This movement caused her breasts to press together, much to Mozart's mischievous amusement.

He also wrote a canon titled "Leck mich im Arsch," which bluntly translates to "Lick me in the ass." After opera singer Aloysia Weber rejected his marriage proposal, Mozart retaliated by improvising a mocking song that included the line, "The one who doesn't like me can lick my ass." In an ironic twist, he later married her younger sister, Constanze.

Mozart's humor frequently leaned towards the obscene. He was known to write vulgar poems to his cousin, one of which included the line, "By the love of my skin, I shit on your nose, so it runs down your chin." Despite his crude humor and eccentricities, Mozart's musical brilliance remains unmatched, securing his place as one of the most influential composers in history.

A FAIRY TALE OF TWO CITIES

Charles Dickens, one of the most acclaimed authors of the 19th century, was born in Hampshire, England, in 1812. Known for novels like Oliver Twist, A Christmas Carol, David Copperfield, A Tale of Two Cities, and Great Expectations, his works captivated audiences worldwide. Among his admirers was Danish writer Hans Christian Andersen, celebrated for his fairy tales, including The Little Mermaid, The Ugly Duckling, and The Emperor's New Clothes.

The two literary giants first met briefly in 1847, sparking a one-sided correspondence as Andersen inundated Dickens with letters expressing admiration. By 1857, Andersen planned to visit England and eagerly accepted Dickens' polite invitation to stay at his home for a night or two. However, what Dickens anticipated as a brief visit turned into an exhausting five-week ordeal.

Upon arrival, Andersen quickly wore out his welcome. He lamented the absence of a personal assistant, even suggesting that Dickens' son shave him each morning. His emotional volatility further strained the household, with frequent dramatic outbursts over minor inconveniences. During one dinner party, Andersen awkwardly linked arms with Dickens as they entered the dining room, leaving guests perplexed.

The most disruptive incident occurred during the premiere of Dickens' play, The Frozen Deep. Feeling ignored by the audience, Andersen erupted into loud sobbing, unsettling attendees, including Queen Victoria. By the end of his stay, the Dickens family was at their wit's end.

After Andersen departed, Dickens scrawled on the guest room mirror: "Hans Andersen slept in this room for five weeks—which seemed to the family AGES!"

Though the visit tested Dickens' patience, it inspired him creatively. Andersen's eccentricities influenced the creation of the character Uriah Heep in David Copperfield. This peculiar visit remains a humorous footnote in literary history, reflecting the complexities of relationships between great artistic minds.

MECHANICAL MESSIAH

John Murray Spear was an abolitionist who played a significant role in leading the Underground Railroad through Boston and was involved in both the abolitionist and women's suffrage movements. However, despite his contributions, Spear's later years were marked by increasingly bizarre behavior. In 1852, he became deeply involved in spiritualism, claiming that the spirits of Thomas Jefferson and Benjamin Franklin had instructed him to introduce a revolutionary new technology that would change the world.

Spear and a small group of followers built what he called a "mechanical Jesus Christ," a device that he believed could power the world through supernatural perpetual motion. To activate the machine, he insisted on a divine intervention, so one of his followers pretended to give birth to the device through an "immaculate conception" in a strange and ritualistic ceremony. Unfortunately, the device didn't work as expected, leading to frustration among his followers, who destroyed the creation.

Despite the failure of his mechanical Jesus, Spear continued with his unorthodox beliefs until his death in 1887. His legacy is a mix of important contributions to social justice and a deeply eccentric spiritual journey.

THEY CALL IT MUMMY LOVE

Carl Tanzler was born in 1877 in Dresden, Germany. From a young age, he experienced vivid visions of an ancestor showing him the face of his destined love—a dark-haired, exotic beauty. This mysterious woman frequently appeared in his dreams, even though Carl had never met her.

In 1926, Carl moved to Florida and settled in Key West the following year, working as a radiology technician. While at the hospital, he met Maria Elena Milagro de Hoyos, a Cuban-American woman being treated for tuberculosis. The moment he saw her, Carl believed she was the woman from his visions and his true love. Obsessed, he offered to provide special treatments at her home, brought her gifts, and even professed his love. Maria, however, did not reciprocate his feelings and succumbed to tuberculosis on October 25, 1931.

Carl paid for Maria's funeral and constructed a mausoleum for her, which he visited nightly for almost two years. Unable to bear her absence, he decided to bring Maria back into his life. In April 1933, he secretly removed her corpse from the mausoleum, using a toy wagon to transport her body to his home. There, Carl attempted to preserve her decaying remains by filling her abdomen with rags, replacing her decomposed skin with wax-coated cloth, and inserting glass eyes. To mask the odor, he applied perfumes and kept the body in his bed.

For years, rumors swirled about Carl's obsession, but no one had proof until October 1940, when Maria's sister visited his home.

Through an open window, she saw Carl dancing with Maria's corpse. Authorities were notified, and Carl was arrested. Though he stood trial, the case was dismissed. Maria's body was reburied, and Carl lived out his days alone. He died on July 3, 1952, at the age of 75, lying next to a wax death mask of Maria.

CHAPTER 2

UNITED STATES HISTORY

BENJAMIN'S BIZZARE LIFE

Born in Boston in 1706, Benjamin Franklin showed remarkable intellectual promise early on, founding The New-England Courant at just fifteen. His personal life was equally eventful; he fathered an illegitimate son, William Franklin, who was born on February 22, 1730. William would later have his own illegitimate son, also named William Franklin, on February 22, 1760—exactly thirty years later.

Franklin considered himself a Renaissance man, possessing a wide range of talents. A gifted writer, he authored Poor Richard's Almanack and made groundbreaking contributions to science, notably his experiments with electricity and the invention of bifocals. His ingenuity extended to music as well—he created the glass harmonica, an instrument that caught the attention of composers such as Mozart and Beethoven.

Though highly intelligent, Franklin also had a mischievous streak and enjoyed teasing his rivals. In one infamous incident, he predicted the death of his competitor, writer Titan Leeds, in Poor Richard's Almanack. When Leeds did not die on the predicted date, Franklin refused to retract his statement, instead claiming that the living Leeds was an imposter, and that the real Titan Leeds had indeed died as foretold.

Despite his playful nature, Franklin became a key figure in the American Revolution. Recognizing that the colonial army stood little chance against the British, the revolutionaries sought French aid, and Franklin was sent to Paris as a diplomat.

Not only did he successfully secure French military support, but he also became a sensation in Parisian society, known for his charm and, infamously, his romantic escapades. Franklin's legendary appetite for pleasure led him to frequent Parisian brothels, where he reportedly contracted several diseases. His views on sex were equally candid in a 1745 letter, he advised young men to pursue older women, arguing that they were more eager to please. He also remarked that women aged "downwards," writing that "the face first grows lank and wrinkled; then the neck; then the breast and arms," humorously adding that "in the dark, all cats are grey."

While in France, Franklin also applied his scientific mind. In 1784, King Louis XVI invited him to join a team of scientists investigating "animal magnetism," a theory proposing that an invisible force within all living beings could be manipulated to heal physical and mental ailments. This theory was promoted by the German doctor Franz Mesmer, who performed procedures to harness this force—a process that became known as being "mesmerized." Franklin worked alongside scientists such as Ignace Guillotin (whose name later became associated with the execution device, though he did not invent it) and Jean Sylvain Bailly (who would later be executed by that very device). Their conclusion was that mesmerism only succeeded when the patient expected it to—marking one of the earliest studies of the placebo effect.

Franklin returned to the United States an international hero, celebrated throughout the colonies, which—thanks in no small part to his efforts—were now on their way to becoming an independent nation. He spent his later years in relative peace and seclusion, only occasionally stepping back into public and political life. He died in Philadelphia on April 17, 1790, just three years after signing the United States Constitution.

OLD AND BOLD

Samuel Whittemore might just be one of the most fearless and resilient figures in American history, yet his name is largely forgotten. Born in 1696 in Charlestown, Massachusetts, he showed his warrior spirit early on, fighting in the French and Indian War at the age of 64.

But his most legendary moment came during the American Revolution in 1775. At 78 years old, Whittemore saw a detachment of British soldiers marching toward his property during the battles of Lexington and Concord. Undeterred by his age, he grabbed his musket and launched a one-man ambush, killing two soldiers before drawing his sword and attacking others at close range.

Outnumbered and outmatched, Whittemore was eventually overpowered. He was shot in the face and stabbed repeatedly with bayonets, left for dead by the British troops. But when colonial soldiers found him, they were stunned to see him still alive—and attempting to reload his musket to keep fighting.

Despite his grievous wounds, Whittemore was taken to a doctor who warned that his survival was impossible. Yet he defied all odds, not only recovering but living for another 18 years. He passed away at the remarkable age of 96, earning his place in history as one of the toughest patriots to ever take the field.

ANNIE, GET YOUR GUN

In an era when women were often excluded from fame and recognition, one remarkable young woman from Darke County, Ohio, shattered societal norms and became a global icon. Born Phoebe Ann Mosey on August 13, 1860, Annie Oakley grew up in a Quaker family and displayed an extraordinary talent for firearms from a young age. By the age of eight, she was hunting game to support her family, and by 15, her sharpshooting skills had earned enough to pay off her mother's mortgage.

Oakley's talent led to her first competition against Frank Butler, a seasoned marksman. Despite being a young woman in a male-dominated field, she narrowly defeated Butler. Their rivalry soon turned into romance, and they married. Together, they joined Buffalo Bill's Wild West Show in 1885, where Oakley became a sensation. She dazzled audiences with feats such as shooting coins in midair, extinguishing candle flames, and hitting playing cards multiple times while they were in flight.

Her incredible skill caught the attention of Lakota Chief Sitting Bull, who believed she possessed supernatural abilities. He gave her the nickname "Little Sure Shot" and gifted her the moccasins he had worn during the Battle of Little Bighorn. Oakley's fame transcended borders, and she performed for European royalty, including Queen Victoria in 1887 and German Prince Wilhelm II. After World War I began, Oakley humorously offered to repeat her stunt of shooting the ashes off Wilhelm's cigarette—this time with a more permanent outcome. The Kaiser never replied. Beyond her sharpshooting fame, Oakley was a trailblazer for women's rights.

During the Spanish-American War, she wrote to President McKinley, offering to lead a team of 50 female sharpshooters, though her proposal was declined. She continued advocating for women in the armed forces and broke barriers as the first female superstar. Oakley performed into her 60s, setting records even at 62 before passing away in 1926.

THE WORLD'S FAIR

In 1893, Chicago hosted the World's Columbian Exposition to commemorate the 400th anniversary of Christopher Columbus's arrival in the Americas. Spanning nearly 700 acres and featuring around 200 buildings, the event—also known as the Chicago World's Fair—drew nearly 30 million visitors from May 5 to October 31. It became a showcase of American ingenuity, global culture, and technological innovation.

One of the fair's most iconic attractions was a giant rotating wheel equipped with passenger cars designed by a man named George Ferris Jr. Another highlight was Nikola Tesla's exhibit of electrical devices, which demonstrated the transformative potential of his inventions and foreshadowed advancements in electricity.

The fair introduced many products and concepts that became cultural staples. Juicy Fruit gum, Cracker Jacks, and Pabst Blue Ribbon beer made their debuts, alongside the "brownie," a dessert created by Bertha Palmer that would go on to gain widespread popularity.

Additionally, the first public performance of the Pledge of Allegiance took place, cementing a new tradition in American life. Guests including Helen Keller and Alexander Graham Bell were entertained by renowned figures such as Scott Joplin, who played his distinctive ragtime music, and John Philip Sousa, who led musical renditions. The Mormon Tabernacle Choir performed outside Utah for the first time, and Erik Weisz, later known as Harry Houdini, dazzled attendees with his magical acts.

THE DARK TRUTH OF POCAHONTAS

Most people's perception of Pocahontas is heavily influenced by the Disney movie, but the true history is far more tragic. When British colonists landed in Virginia, they were under the leadership of Governor Ratcliffe, similar to how it's portrayed in the film. John Smith, one of the colonists, was captured by Chief Powhatan, but the resemblance to the animated tale stops there. Although Smith later claimed that Pocahontas saved his life, historical accounts suggest he was never in real danger. In reality, Pocahontas was only 11 years old at the time, and there was no romantic relationship between her and Smith—his story was likely fabricated to enhance his own legend.

At 17, Pocahontas was taken captive by the English. She married a colonist named John Rolfe and was brought to England, where she was exhibited as a "civilized" Native woman to high society. Tragically, she died at just 20 years old, three years after her arrival in England.

The fate of Governor Ratcliffe was far more brutal than what the movie suggests. Contrary to the film's version, where he is merely imprisoned by his own men, the real

Ratcliffe was captured by Powhatan's warriors. He endured a horrifying death—his skin was peeled off and thrown into a fire before his eyes, leaving him to die in excruciating pain.

NOBLE NELLIE

In the 1880s, journalist Nellie Bly persuaded Joseph Pulitzer, the owner of the New York World, to allow her to investigate the treatment of patients in mental asylums. She proposed a daring plan: to feign insanity and get herself committed to a mental hospital, enabling her to report on the conditions from within. Bly checked into a boarding house and convincingly acted deranged, leading the staff to have her admitted to Blackwell's Island Mental Hospital.

Inside the asylum, she witnessed and documented appalling conditions, including abuse, neglect, and mistreatment of patients. After ten days, she revealed her true identity as a journalist, expecting to be released. To her shock, the guards refused to believe her, forcing her to remain in the asylum for several more days. It wasn't until Joseph Pulitzer intervened that she was finally freed.

Upon her release, Bly wrote Ten Days in a Mad-House, exposing the horrific realities within mental institutions. Her groundbreaking investigative journalism ignited public outrage and spurred calls for reform, bringing much-needed attention to the cruel practices occurring within the mental health system. Her courage and determination not only challenged societal norms but also paved the way for future investigative reporting.

EDISON AND THE ELEPHANT

In 1903, a circus elephant named Topsy killed a spectator in New York, prompting plans for her execution. Initially, the circus proposed a public hanging, intending to sell tickets to the gruesome event. However, the ASPCA intervened, halting the hanging but not Topsy's impending death. Amid the controversy, inventor Thomas Edison saw an opportunity to use Topsy's execution for a different purpose.

Edison, embroiled in a rivalry with Nikola Tesla over the superiority of their electrical systems, sought to discredit Tesla's alternating current (AC) by demonstrating its lethality. He requested permission to execute Topsy as part of a short film he planned to produce. Metal shoes were fitted to Topsy, and she was led onto an electrified platform. Edison then sent 6,600 volts of AC through her body, killing her instantly as smoke rose from her lifeless form.

Edison filmed the entire event, releasing it as a short, titled Electrocuting an Elephant. His aim was to persuade the public that AC, Tesla's system, was inherently dangerous compared to his own direct current (DC).

Topsy's death, framed as a safety demonstration, became a dark chapter in the so-called "War of the Currents." While Edison's propaganda effort ultimately failed to eliminate AC, the exploitation of Topsy's tragic fate remains a haunting example of the lengths to which ambition and rivalry can extend.

THE CULT AND THE ASSASSIN

The Oneida Community was founded in 1848 by John Humphrey Noyes in Oneida, New York, initially with 87 members. By 1878, its population grew to over 300. The community aimed to support itself by manufacturing products, starting with silverware in 1877. The group disbanded in 1881, but eventually became Oneida Limited, a successful silverware manufacturer still in operation today.

The community was known for its radical beliefs, including the concept of "free love," which Noyes coined. They rejected traditional monogamy and practiced communal relationships, where older women, past childbearing age, would act as sexual mentors to young boys. These women were tasked with teaching the boys about sex to prevent pregnancies. Additionally, the community believed in selective breeding and eugenics, and men were taught to avoid ejaculation during sex. In 1860, Charles Guiteau joined the cult, claiming that an "irresistible power" led him there. However, the women showed no interest in him, so he left after three years. Guiteau then became involved in politics, supporting Horace Greeley in the 1872 presidential race.

His behavior became erratic, and after James A. Garfield's election in 1880, Guiteau believed he was responsible for him becoming the President of the United States and expected a consulship in Paris. When he was denied, he decided it was his duty to assassinate Garfield to save the Republican Party.

On July 2, 1881, Guiteau shot President Garfield at a Washington, D.C. train station. Garfield was treated for weeks, but despite efforts like using Alexander Graham Bell's metal detector, he died on September 19, 1881.

THE HIPPO BILL

In 1910, the United States faced a severe meat shortage, leading government leaders to explore unconventional solutions. One of the most unusual proposals came from Louisiana representative Robert Broussard, who suggested importing large numbers of hippos from Africa to populate the bayous of Louisiana. He believed that these hippos could provide thousands of pounds of fresh meat, helping to solve the country's food crisis.

This bold idea, known as the American Hippo Bill, gained surprising traction, receiving support from influential figures, including President Theodore Roosevelt and the Department of Agriculture. Even The New York Times endorsed the proposal, referring to hippo meat as "lake cow bacon."

To bring this vision to life, Broussard enlisted the help of two remarkable men: Frederick Russell Burnham, a key figure in the early development of the Boy Scouts, and Fritz Duquesne. Adding a twist to the story, Burnham and Duquesne were former enemies who had fought on opposite sides during the Boer War in South Africa.

In fact, they were once tasked with assassinating each other—a mission that neither carried out. Despite the intriguing and imaginative nature of the proposal, the American Hippo Bill ultimately failed to pass, and the idea of hippo ranching in Louisiana faded into history.

MCNAIR AND SPACE

Ronald McNair, born on October 21st, 1950, in Lake City, South Carolina, grew up in a time and place where racial segregation made education a significant challenge for African Americans. At the age of 8, McNair encountered discrimination when he attempted to check out books from the Lake City Public Library, only to be refused by the librarian because of his race. Undeterred, young Ronald stayed until the police arrived, forcing the librarian to comply and check out the books. This early experience of standing up for his rights foreshadowed the resilience that would define his life.

McNair went on to excel academically, graduating as valedictorian in 1967 and later earning a degree in engineering. In 1976, he earned a PhD in physics from MIT. His academic achievements led him to NASA, where in 1978 he was selected as one of 35 applicants for the astronaut program, thanks to the efforts of Star Trek actress Nichelle Nichols. In 1984, McNair became the second African American to fly into space.

Tragically, on January 28, 1986, McNair's life was cut short when the Challenger space shuttle exploded shortly after launch, killing him and six other crew members, including teacher Christa McAuliffe. Despite his untimely death, McNair's legacy has endured, with numerous buildings and monuments named in his honor. The Lake City Public Library, once the site of his childhood protest, is now the Ronald E. McNair Life History Center, a testament to his extraordinary life and achievements.

GERONIMO THE INVINCIBLE

Geronimo, born on June 16th, 1829, in present-day New Mexico, is a name synonymous with bravery and legendary feats. Raised in the Apache tradition, his life was filled with extraordinary events that contributed to his mystique. One of the most tragic and pivotal moments occurred in 1851 when 400 Mexican soldiers attacked his home camp, killing his wife and three children. Seeking revenge, Geronimo fought fiercely alongside Chokonen leader Cochise, and during a raid, he reportedly stabbed several Mexican soldiers while avoiding gunfire, fueling the belief that he possessed supernatural powers.

A skilled medicine man, Geronimo was believed to have the ability to heal, manipulate time, and even be invincible to bullets. His visions were also considered prophetic, such as when he foresaw an attack on his camp by U.S. forces, which tragically came true. Geronimo's relentless battles against both Mexican and American troops made him one of the most wanted men in U.S. history. In 1886, after years of pursuit, he and his men surrendered and were imprisoned.

Geronimo's later years took an unexpected turn as he became a living spectacle, appearing at world fairs and posing for photos as the "Apache Terror." Despite his fame and celebrity status, he remained a prisoner of war until his death from pneumonia on February 17, 1909.

Adding to the intrigue of his story are dark rumors that his grave was desecrated by members of Yale's secretive Skull and Bones society, allegedly including a young Prescott Bush—father of President George H.W. Bush and grandfather of President George W. Bush. According to legend, Geronimo's skull was stolen and is now kept as a relic within the society's mysterious "Tomb." Today, Geronimo is remembered not only as a fierce warrior but also as a powerful symbol of resistance and defiance against oppression.

TEDDY'S KIDS

Teddy Roosevelt, the 26th President of the United States, made history as the youngest person to ever hold the office at that time. Renowned for his toughness and unwavering grit, Roosevelt demonstrated remarkable courage throughout his military and political careers. His spirit of tenacity and fearlessness was deeply ingrained in his children, who inherited his boldness and integrity, never shying away from being their authentic selves or confronting challenges head-on.

When Teddy Roosevelt became president in 1901, his daughter, Alice Roosevelt, quickly captured the nation's attention, becoming a celebrated socialite. Known for defying societal norms, Alice charmed Americans with her boldness during an era when women were expected to conform. She openly gambled on sports, smoked cigarettes on the White House roof, and even owned an unconventional pet—a snake named Emily.

Alice's sharp wit and unfiltered opinions only added to her notoriety. She once famously quipped that her father, the President of the United States, wanted "to be the bride at every wedding and the corpse at every funeral." When confronted about Alice's wild antics, President Roosevelt reportedly remarked, "I can either run the country or tend to Alice, but I cannot possibly do both." Her unpredictable behavior became legendary, solidifying her reputation as a trailblazer for independent women.

As Roosevelt's presidency ended and William Howard Taft prepared to take office, Alice left her mark in a truly unforgettable way.

In a final act of mischief, she crafted a voodoo doll of the incoming first lady, Nellie Taft, and buried it in the White House yard. This bold farewell was perfectly in character for the unconventional first daughter, whose antics have become a vivid chapter in the history of the Roosevelt family and the White House. Alice's unapologetic individuality and rebellious spirit cemented her status as one of the most fascinating figures of her era.

The legacy of boldness in the Roosevelt family did not end with Alice. On D-Day, June 6, 1944, over 150,000 Allied soldiers stormed the beaches of Normandy. Among them was General Theodore Roosevelt Jr., the son of former President Teddy Roosevelt. At 56 years old, he was the oldest person to participate in the invasion and the only general whose son was landing on the beaches alongside him that day.

Refusing to remain safely in the rear, General Roosevelt chose to land with the first wave of troops. Bravely standing in the line of fire, he directed soldiers to safety and helped them navigate the chaos of battle, narrowly dodging bullets along the way. Just one month later, while resting in a captured German truck in France, he suffered a heart attack and died.

Theodore Roosevelt Jr.'s courage and leadership on D-Day earned him the Medal of Honor, a testament to the fearless spirit passed down from his father. Together, Alice and Theodore Jr. embodied the boldness and independence that defined the Roosevelt family, leaving a legacy of audacity and strength that continues to inspire.

United States History

CHAPTER 3

CRAZY COINCIDENCES

TED HINTON AND THE WAITRESS

Ted Hinton was born on October 5, 1904, in Dallas, Texas, where he grew up and became acquainted with Clyde Barrow, a fellow Dallas native. This early connection would later lead to one of the most dramatic events of Hinton's life.

In 1932, Hinton became a deputy sheriff in Dallas and frequently visited Marco's Café, where he developed a fondness for a beautiful waitress. They often chatted, and she seemed to enjoy his company. One day, however, she vanished without explanation, leaving Hinton puzzled.

A few years later, Hinton was assigned to assist Texas Ranger Frank Hamer in tracking down Clyde Barrow, who, alongside his partner Bonnie Parker, was on a violent 21-month crime spree. The couple's exploits left 13 people dead, including nine police officers, earning them infamy during an era dominated by criminals like John Dillinger and Pretty Boy Floyd.

By May 1934, Hamer had spent months studying Bonnie and Clyde's movements. His efforts led him to northwest Louisiana, where he learned the couple planned to visit the Methvin family. On May 23, 1934, Hamer's posse, which included Hinton, set an ambush on Louisiana State Highway 154.

That morning, Bonnie and Clyde's car approached at high speed but slowed when blocked by a truck. As the car decelerated, the six-man posse opened fire, unleashing 130 rounds.

Clyde was killed instantly by a headshot, while Bonnie's screams echoed as bullets riddled the vehicle. Clyde was struck 17 times; Bonnie, 26.

When the gunfire ceased, Hinton approached the bullet-riddled car. Amid the carnage lay Clyde Barrow, his childhood acquaintance, and Bonnie Parker—the beautiful waitress he had once admired at Marco's Café.

A CRAZY DAM COINCIDENCE

Completed in 1936, the Hoover Dam rises 726 feet and stretches 1,244 feet across, constructed from 4.3 million cubic yards of concrete—enough to pave a 16-foot-wide road from New York City to Seattle. It has since become an iconic symbol of American resilience.

The construction of the dam was grueling and dangerous. Starting in April 1931, amidst a scorching heatwave, temperatures in the construction tunnels soared to 140 degrees. Out of the 20,000 workers, 96 men lost their lives in accidents. One of the most poignant and eerie coincidences in American history occurred during the dam's construction.

On December 20, 1921, surveyor John George Tierney was killed in a flash flood while assessing the site, making John Tierney the first person to die during the construction of the Hoover Dam. Throughout the following fourteen years, over 90 more workers would die during the dam's construction. On December 20, 1935, a 25-year-old man fell 320 feet to his death during the dam's construction, becoming the last person to die during the construction of the dam.

That final victim was a young man named Patrick Tierney, the son of John George Tierney. The father and son both tragically lost their lives exactly 14 years apart—John first, and Patrick last—marking the beginning and end of the Hoover Dam's deadly toll.

LIKE FATHER, LIKE SON

In 1951, Pakistan's Prime Minister Liaquat Ali Khan was assassinated while delivering a speech at Municipal Park in Rawalpindi. Following his tragic death, the park was renamed Liaquat Bagh in his honor. A doctor named Sadiq Khan attempted to save his life but was ultimately unsuccessful.

Fifty-six years later, history repeated itself in a chillingly similar way. On December 27, 2007, Prime Minister Benazir Bhutto attended a political rally at Liaquat Bagh. As she was leaving the event, an assassin detonated a bomb near her vehicle. Gravely injured, Bhutto was rushed to the same hospital where Liaquat Ali Khan had been taken decades earlier. Despite the medical team's best efforts, she too succumbed to her injuries.

In an extraordinary twist of fate, the doctor who tried to save Bhutto, Mohammad Khan, was the son of Sadiq Khan—the same doctor who had fought to save Liaquat Ali Khan's life. This tragic connection underscores a haunting chapter in Pakistan's history, as two of its most influential leaders were assassinated at the same location, generations apart, despite the passage of time.

POE'S PREDICTIONS

Edgar Allan Poe, who passed away under mysterious circumstances in 1849, is widely regarded as a cornerstone of gothic literature, celebrated for his horror-filled tales and exploration of human fears. He is credited with inventing the modern detective story and revolutionizing science fiction. Poe's influence on American literature remains undeniable, with his 69 short stories and one novel, The Narrative of Arthur Gordon Pym of Nantucket (1838), standing as notable works.

In The Narrative of Arthur Gordon Pym, Poe tells the story of a crew stranded at sea after their ship, the Grampus, sinks. As their survival chances dwindle, they draw lots to determine who will be sacrificed to feed the rest. The unlucky "winner" is Richard Parker, who is then killed and eaten by the crew.

Remarkably, 45 years later, a similar tragedy occurred. In 1884, the Mignonette, a ship bound for Australia, was sunk off the coast of South Africa. Four crew members survived, but one, a 17-year-old cabin, fell ill. With no other choice, the remaining crew killed and ate him.

After being rescued, the three men were tried for murder, and their sentences were reduced. The name of that 17-year-old cabin boy was Richard Parker.

The coincidence of both Richard Parkers meeting similar fates—one fictional and one real—raises questions of fate or clairvoyance.

This incredible event would later inspire Yann Martel's Life of Pi, where a shipwrecked boy is accompanied by a Bengal tiger named Richard Parker.

THE LIFE OF GEORGE STORY

In 1936, LIFE Magazine launched its first issue, choosing to feature the birth of a random American baby as a symbolic representation of new beginnings. The idea was to periodically update readers on this child's life, creating a unique narrative thread that would grow alongside the publication.

The baby chosen for this role was a boy named George Story. Throughout the years, LIFE Magazine followed his journey, sharing significant milestones and life events with its readers.

In 2000, LIFE Magazine announced it would cease publication. Remarkably, shortly after this announcement, George Story passed away. In a poignant twist of fate, the magazine that began with his birth concluded its own story just as his life came to an end, bringing the narrative full circle in a way no one could have predicted.

LUCY'S LOVERS

Lucy Hale, born in 1841, was the daughter of a U.S. Senator and well-known for her charm and numerous admirers. Among them was Robert Todd Lincoln, the son of Abraham Lincoln, who would become the 16th President of the United States. Both Lucy's and Robert's fathers hoped the two would marry, but their relationship never moved beyond close friendship.

In 1862, Lucy received a letter from a mysterious admirer expressing a desire to court her. The admirer revealed himself, and the two began a romantic relationship. Lucy and her new beau grew close, and she even secured him a ticket to attend Abraham Lincoln's second inauguration, a historic event at which her friend Robert Todd Lincoln was also present.

On April 14, 1865, Lucy spent time with Robert Todd Lincoln before departing to meet her admirer. After a brief visit with Lucy, the man excused himself, explaining he had plans to attend the theater. Her admirer was a highly celebrated actor of the time who would become infamous that very evening for assassinating Abraham Lincoln at Ford's Theatre.

Unbeknownst to Lucy until that fateful night, the man she had been romantically involved with, John Wilkes Booth, was plotting one of the most consequential acts in American history. The revelation left her forever tied to the tragic and shocking events surrounding Lincoln's assassination, casting a shadow over her life and legacy.

A TITANIC PREDICTION

Author Morgan Robertson is best known for his novella Futility, which tells the story of the sinking of the largest passenger ship ever built after it strikes an iceberg in the North Atlantic. In his tale, the doomed vessel is named the Titan.

On April 15, 1912, the British passenger liner RMS Titanic met a strikingly similar fate, colliding with an iceberg and sinking, leading to the deaths of approximately 1,500 people. The tragedy remains one of the most infamous maritime disasters in history.

What makes this even more astonishing is that Robertson wrote Futility in 1898—fourteen years before the Titanic disaster occurred. The eerie parallels between his fictional Titan and the real-life Titanic continue to baffle readers, earning Robertson a place in history as the author who seemingly predicted one of the greatest maritime tragedies of all time.

A CRAZY CIVIL WAR COINCIDENCE

The first major battle of the Civil War, the Battle of Bull Run, took place near Manassas, Virginia, in July 1861, on the property of a grocer named Wilmer McLean. His house, located at the heart of the battlefield, was severely damaged, with a cannonball even crashing through his fireplace. Hoping to protect his family from the chaos of war, McLean moved them 120 miles south in 1863 to a quiet area he believed would be safe from further conflict.

Ironically, his attempt to escape the war led him right back into its path. On April 9, 1865, Confederate General Robert E. Lee met Union General Ulysses S. Grant to surrender, effectively ending the Civil War. The site chosen for this historic meeting was none other than McLean's new home in Appomattox Court House, Virginia.

In a remarkable twist of fate, the Civil War both began and ended on property owned by Wilmer McLean. His story illustrates how the war reached every corner of American life, even touching those who tried to avoid it.

Today, McLean is remembered as a symbol of history's strange coincidences, linking the first and last chapters of the nation's most defining conflict

OH, BROTHER!

During the Prohibition era of the 1920s, federal agents were tasked with curbing the illegal production and sale of alcohol—a dangerous job that often involved violent confrontations. Among these agents was Richard James Hart, a sharpshooting lawman from Nebraska. Nicknamed "Two-Gun" Hart for his success in raiding bootleggers, he earned a fearsome reputation as one of Prohibition's most effective enforcers.

Hart's journey to law enforcement began long before Prohibition. In 1916, he served in the U.S. military under General John J. Pershing during the mission to capture Mexican revolutionary Pancho Villa. Although the mission failed, Hart gained valuable combat experience. After World War I, he settled in Homer, Nebraska, where he became the town marshal. By 1920, he had transitioned into federal service as a Prohibition agent.

Hart's skills led to his appointment as a special agent for the Bureau of Indian Affairs, where he dismantled bootlegging operations on the Cheyenne River Indian Reservation in South Dakota. His impressive work earned him a prestigious role as a security guard for President Calvin Coolidge during a 1927 visit to the reservation.

Meanwhile, in Chicago, another figure was rising to infamy: Al Capone. As the leader of America's largest criminal empire, Capone's bootlegging operations earned him an estimated $60 million annually (equivalent to $900 million today).

Despite their seemingly opposing roles in law enforcement and crime, Hart and Capone shared a surprising connection. Richard James Hart was not his real name. Born James Vincenzo Capone in 1892 in Salerno, Italy, Hart was Al Capone's older brother. The two men—one a lawman, the other a notorious gangster—took dramatically different paths in life, creating a complex and ironic family legacy.

CURSE OF THE PRESIDENT'S SON

Robert Todd Lincoln, born August 1st, 1843, was the first son of Abraham Lincoln, the 16th President of the United States, and Mary Todd. He was the only child of the Lincolns to survive past the age of 18; his brothers Edward, William, and Tad all died young. While Robert lived into adulthood, death seemed to follow him throughout his life. At the age of 20, Robert nearly died in a train accident in Jersey City, New Jersey, but was saved by a man who later turned out to be Edwin Booth, the brother of his father's assassin, John Wilkes Booth.

Robert served as an officer in the Union Army during the Civil War, ultimately witnessing General Lee's surrender at Appomattox. On April 14th, 1865, Robert declined his parents' invitation to attend the theater at Ford's Theatre, where his father was assassinated by John Wilkes Booth. In 1871, Robert's brother Tad died of tuberculosis, leaving Robert to care for his mentally unstable mother.

In 1881, Robert became Secretary of War under President James Garfield. On July 2nd of that year, he witnessed Garfield's assassination by Charles Guiteau at a Washington, D.C. train station, becoming the second president in his lifetime to be murdered. Afterward, Robert stepped back from politics, taking a position with the Pullman Palace Car Company.

In 1901, Robert visited President William McKinley at the Pan-American Exposition in Buffalo, New York, where McKinley was shot by an anarchist. McKinley's wounds would later prove fatal.

This marked the third presidential assassination in Robert's life. He spent his final years in private life, passing away on July 26th, 1926, at the age of 82.

CHAPTER 4

BRUSHING SHOULDERS WITH THE NAZIS

HE AIN'T HEAVY, HE'S MEIN BRUDER

Rudolf and Adolf Dassler were born in Bavaria, Germany, in 1898 and 1900, respectively. In 1919, the brothers founded a shoe company called Geda, which quickly gained recognition on the global stage. During the 1936 Berlin Olympics, they convinced American track star Jesse Owens to wear their Geda shoes while competing. Owens went on to win four gold medals, all while wearing the Dassler brothers' shoes—a triumphant moment that reportedly infuriated Adolf Hitler, as both brothers were members of the Nazi Party.

When World War II began in 1939, Rudolf was drafted into the German army, and their shoe factory was converted into a weapons manufacturing facility. Tensions between the brothers grew over the years, ultimately leading to a bitter split in 1948. Geda was dissolved, and Rudolf founded his own shoe company, originally named Ruda. Just one year later, Adolf established his own brand, using his nickname, Adi Dassler, to create Adidas.

In 1950, Rudolf rebranded Ruda as Puma, setting the stage for an intense rivalry between the two brothers.

This fierce competition not only divided their hometown of Herzogenaurach but also helped shape the global sportswear industry. Today, Adidas and Puma stand as two of the most iconic sports brands in the world, born from a family feud that changed the landscape of athletic footwear forever.

THE PIONEER OF PROPAGANDA

When you think of breakfast, bacon and eggs likely come to mind. But this classic combination wasn't always the go-to morning meal. The trend of eating bacon for breakfast began in the 1920s when a meat company hired Edward Bernays, a pioneer in public relations, to boost bacon sales. Bernays revolutionized advertising by using strategic propaganda, earning him the title "father of public relations." His innovative techniques reshaped consumer behavior and attracted major clients, including General Electric, CBS, and the American Tobacco Company.

Bernays wasn't just influential in advertising—he also played a significant role in changing social norms. Noticing that women generally didn't smoke, he launched a campaign that portrayed cigarettes as "torches of freedom," cleverly linking smoking to women's liberation. This tactic successfully encouraged women to take up smoking. Ironically, despite knowing the health risks associated with cigarettes, Bernays privately mocked his own wife for her smoking habit.

In a dark twist of history, Nazi propaganda minister Joseph Goebbels studied and admired Bernays' methods, using them to craft the Nazi party's messaging. The irony is profound—Bernays was Jewish and the nephew of Sigmund Freud, a renowned psychoanalyst and outspoken critic of the Nazis.

Edward Bernays' legacy is a complex one. He not only transformed advertising and public relations but also demonstrated the power of propaganda in shaping public opinion. His influence extended beyond the commercial world, leaving a lasting impact on political communication and social behavior.

HEIL HENRY

Henry Ford, the founder of the Ford Motor Company, transformed the automobile industry with his innovative moving assembly line, which reduced the production time of a Model T from 12 hours to just 90 minutes. His factories produced about 10,000 cars daily, and he famously doubled his workers' wages, helping to create a new American middle class.

However, despite his industrial achievements, Ford was also known for his staunch antisemitism. In 1920, he began publishing a weekly magazine called The International Jew: The World's Problem, which disseminated harmful antisemitic propaganda.

These writings found an audience in Austria, influencing a young Adolf Hitler, who mentioned Ford by name in his manifesto, Mein Kampf, making Ford the only American praised in the book. Ford's antisemitic publications were even used as ideological tools by the Nazis, being cited during the Nuremberg Trials as part of the indoctrination of Nazi Youth.

In acknowledgment of his influence and shared ideology, Ford received the Grand Cross of the German Eagle, the highest honor awarded to foreigners by Nazi Germany, directly from Hitler himself.

THE BRAVE LITTLE WARRIOR

When Nazi forces invaded the Soviet Union, 16-year-old Zinaida Portnova joined the Belarusian Resistance Movement, dedicating herself to the fight against the occupation. Initially, she assisted by collecting weapons for Soviet forces and sabotaging Nazi operations, including using explosives to destroy Nazi-controlled factories in Belarus.

In 1943, Zinaida took a position working in a kitchen that prepared food for Nazi troops. Seizing the opportunity, she poisoned the food supply, resulting in numerous Nazi casualties. When suspicion fell on her, Zinaida boldly ate the poisoned food to prove her innocence. Despite ingesting the toxic meal, she initially displayed no symptoms, convincing the Nazis of her innocence and avoiding immediate capture. Once released, however, she became violently ill but managed to recover.

Later that year, her activities as a resistance fighter came to light, leading to her arrest by the Gestapo. During an interrogation, Zinaida demonstrated her fearless determination by grabbing her interrogator's gun, shooting and killing him. She also killed two guards before fleeing into the wilderness.

Her escape was short-lived, as she was recaptured by the Gestapo. Despite being subjected to brutal torture, she refused to betray her comrades or divulge any information.

On January 15, 1944, Zinaida Portnova was executed at just 17 years old. Her courage, resourcefulness, and unwavering resistance made her a symbol of youthful defiance and sacrifice in the face of tyranny.

G MARKS THE SPOT

Ernst Gräfenberg was a German physician who rose to prominence as a gynecologist during World War I. In 1929, he transformed reproductive health by inventing the Gräfenberg ring, the first intrauterine device (IUD). His pioneering work earned him respect in the medical community, but his life took a perilous turn during World War II.

As a Jewish man in Nazi Germany, Gräfenberg hoped his connections to the wives of high-ranking Nazi officials—many of whom were his patients—would shield him from persecution. However, his confidence proved misplaced. In 1937, he was arrested by the Nazis and imprisoned. His freedom was eventually secured through the intervention of Margaret Sanger, an influential American birth control activist and the future founder of Planned Parenthood, who paid for his release.

Beyond his advancements in contraception, Gräfenberg is celebrated for his research on female sexuality. He identified and studied a sensitive area within the vagina, which was later named the G-Spot in his honor.

Today, Ernst Gräfenberg is remembered as a trailblazer in gynecology and sexual health, whose innovations continue to influence the field

LOCO COCO

Gabrielle "Coco" Chanel, born in Saumur, France, in 1883, was a revolutionary French fashion designer whose innovations transformed women's fashion in the 20th century. As the founder of the Chanel brand her contributions to fashion are continuously celebrated even though her life was marred by controversy, particularly her ties to Nazi Germany during World War II.

In the 1920s, Chanel cultivated relationships within British high society, befriending figures such as Winston Churchill and the Duke of Westminster. Her connection to the duke, an outspoken antisemite, hinted at shared prejudices that later shaped her wartime actions. During this era, Chanel's empire flourished, with her designs reshaping fashion and Chanel No. 5 becoming an enduring fragrance icon.

When World War II began in 1939, Chanel closed her Parisian fashion shops and moved into the Hotel Ritz, where she began a relationship with Baron Hans Günther von Dincklage, a German intelligence agent. This relationship granted her access to Nazi leadership, which she used to pursue personal and financial gain.

Chanel attempted to take control of Parfums Chanel, then owned by the Jewish Wertheimer family, leveraging her Nazi connections to displace them. However, the Wertheimers anticipated her moves and safeguarded their interests. Her actions reflected a willingness to exploit the occupation for her benefit.

Chanel's collaboration deepened in 1941 when she became a Nazi intelligence agent under Walter Schellenberg. She undertook missions, including a failed 1943 effort in Madrid to negotiate Nazi surrender terms with the British ambassador, a friend of Churchill.

Despite her collaboration, Chanel was never prosecuted, reportedly shielded by her friendship with Churchill. After the war, she fled to Switzerland with von Dincklage, returning to fashion in the 1950s to rebuild her brand into a global luxury powerhouse. Today, Chanel is a $25 billion empire, but Coco Chanel's complex legacy includes both brilliance and controversy.

CHAPTER 5

PRESIDENTS AND LEADERS

THE VICE'S VICES

Abraham Lincoln, celebrated as one of America's greatest leaders and orators, remains a towering figure in history for his eloquence and inspiring speeches. However, his vice president, Andrew Johnson, stood in stark contrast to Lincoln in character and public perception—as was glaringly evident during Lincoln's second inauguration on March 4, 1865.

That morning, Johnson, already notorious for his excessive drinking, consumed three large glasses of whiskey one after the other, capping off a week-long binge. His intoxication became painfully apparent during the Senate Chamber ceremony, where he was tasked with delivering his inaugural address. What followed was a rambling, incoherent speech that quickly descended into chaos. Johnson insulted foreign dignitaries and veered into nonsensical tangents, prompting former Vice President Hannibal Hamlin to tug at his coat in an effort to rein him in. When Lincoln entered the chamber amid this debacle, he sat quietly, head bowed in visible embarrassment.

Johnson's drunken state rendered him unable to perform his official duties, including swearing in the incoming senators, a responsibility hastily reassigned to Secretary of the Senate John Forney. Many hoped this public humiliation would mark the end of Johnson's missteps, but fate had other plans.

Less than two months later, on April 14, 1865, Lincoln was assassinated by John Wilkes Booth while attending a play at Ford's Theatre in Washington, D.C.

That same night, a coordinated attack targeted Lincoln's inner circle. Secretary of State William Seward was brutally stabbed in his home by Lewis Powell but survived, while George Atzerodt, assigned to kill Johnson, lost his nerve and roamed the streets of Washington drunk instead.

The next morning, Lincoln succumbed to his injuries, and Johnson unexpectedly assumed the presidency. His tenure, plagued by scandals and failures, is widely regarded as one of the worst in American history. Johnson's impeachment in 1868 cemented his place as a deeply flawed leader, offering a stark and poignant contrast to the legacy of his predecessor, Abraham Lincoln.

FREDERICK THE CURIOUS

Frederick II was crowned Holy Roman Emperor in 1220 and proclaimed himself King of Jerusalem in 1225, a bold move that sent shockwaves across Europe and greatly expanded his influence. His ruthless ambition and controversial actions earned him the title of "Antichrist" from Pope Gregory IX—a condemnation that seemed fitting given his notorious deeds.

Frederick possessed a dark curiosity for human experimentation, a fascination shared by many Germans of his era. In one of his most macabre experiments, he confined an individual in a casket with a small hole at the top, hoping to observe whether the soul would escape through the opening as the person slowly starved to death.

His cruel curiosity extended to language deprivation experiments on infants. He isolated newborns from all human interaction to see if they would spontaneously develop language, believing that this might reveal the original language spoken by Adam and Eve.

These inhumane experiments were driven by his obsessive quest for knowledge, further cementing his reputation as a powerful but feared ruler whose brilliance was matched only by his madness.

HAIL CESAR

Cesar Chavez was a prominent labor leader who co-founded the United Farm Workers (UFW) union in the 1960s, championing the rights of farm workers and advocating for better working conditions. However, Chavez was also heavily influenced by Charles Dedrich, the leader of the Synanon cult, whose teachings left a significant mark on his leadership style. Chavez spent time at the Synanon compound and incorporated some of its practices into the UFW's organizational culture.

One of the practices adopted involved publicly singling out members for harsh verbal criticism, where others would shout insults as a method of humiliation. Under Chavez's leadership, the UFW began to exhibit cult-like traits, including a strict expectation for members to wear UFW buttons at all times as a symbol of loyalty. Chavez also claimed to have healing abilities and required members to work as unpaid "volunteer laborers," with all the revenue generated being controlled by him. This money was later used to pay legal fees following several suspicious deaths of former UFW members who had left the organization.

During the 1980s, Chavez's focus shifted to real estate as he began purchasing apartment complexes and becoming a landlord. Despite his history as a champion for labor rights, he hired only non-union workers to handle renovations on his properties, contradicting his earlier advocacy for unionized labor.

Cesar Chavez's legacy as a labor leader is complex, marked by his significant contributions to workers' rights as well as controversial leadership practices that have sparked debate about his influence and impact on the UFW.

GROVER, I HARDLY KNOW HER

Before running for President in 1884, Grover Cleveland met Maria Halpin and asked her out on a date, to which she agreed. After the date, he walked her to her apartment and asked to come inside. When she refused, Cleveland became increasingly insistent until he forced his way into her apartment and assaulted her.

Six weeks later, Maria discovered she was pregnant with Cleveland's child. Concerned that the scandal could ruin his presidential ambitions, Cleveland had Maria committed to a mental institution, falsely claiming she was mentally unstable despite no supporting evidence. After she gave birth, her child was taken from her and placed in an orphanage.

Despite these events, Grover Cleveland went on to serve two non-consecutive terms as President of the United States. During his presidency, he married Frances Folsom, the daughter of his late best friend, Oscar Folsom. Cleveland had known Frances since she was an infant—27 years before he married her, making her the youngest First Lady in U.S. history

GRANT'S GUARDIAN ANGEL

Ulysses S. Grant, the legendary Civil War hero and commander of Union forces, is best remembered for his pivotal role in General Robert E. Lee's surrender at Appomattox Court House. After his distinguished military career, Grant went on to serve as the 18th President of the United States. However, following his presidency, Grant made a poor financial decision by investing in an investment firm run by his son's friends. Unbeknownst to him, the firm was a massive pyramid scheme, and Grant lost nearly all of his fortune, leaving him with just $80.

Word of his financial ruin spread, and soon people from across the country began sending Grant envelopes of money to help him. Shortly after, Grant was diagnosed with terminal throat cancer. Despite his declining health, Grant had been working on his memoirs and was encouraged by his friend, Samuel Clemens (better known as Mark Twain), to publish them to help alleviate his financial burdens. Twain believed the memoirs could be a success, and he was right. He helped secure the publication of 100,000 advanced copies, providing Grant with some relief knowing his family would be taken care of.

Grant finished his memoirs and passed away just seven days later. Twain's efforts proved fruitful, with the book selling 300,000 copies, even surpassing the sales of Twain's own Huckleberry Finn. Grant's memoirs became a posthumous success, offering both financial relief and a lasting literary legacy.

DOOMED FROM THE START

Charles II ruled Spain from 1661 to 1700 and is widely regarded as one of the most ineffective monarchs in European history. His reign marked the end of the powerful Habsburg dynasty, but his failure as a leader was largely due to his tragic genetic inheritance.

Charles II was born to Philip IV of Spain and Mariana of Austria—an uncle and niece whose own parents were first cousins. This extensive inbreeding within the Habsburg family led to severe physical and cognitive impairments for Charles. It was said that "from the day of his birth, they were waiting for his death," reflecting the grim expectations surrounding his life.

His development was significantly delayed. Charles couldn't speak until he was four and did not learn to walk until he was eight. Even at the age of ten, he was treated as an infant due to his severe disabilities.

When Charles II died, his autopsy revealed shocking physical abnormalities. His heart was reportedly the size of a peppercorn, his lungs were completely corroded, his intestines were rotten and gangrenous, and his head was filled with fluid. He was also discovered to have a single testicle that was described as "black as coal."

The tragic story of Charles II illustrates the devastating consequences of generations of inbreeding, marking the end of the Spanish Habsburg line and a period of decline for the Spanish empire.

PIERCE'S PAINS

By the time Franklin Pierce was elected President in 1852, he and his wife, Jane, had already faced the devastating loss of two of their three sons to illness—one at just four years old and the other as an infant. Their only surviving child was their 11-year-old son, Benjamin.

In 1853, just days before Pierce's inauguration, the family was traveling by train from Massachusetts to New Hampshire when disaster struck—the train derailed. Although Franklin and Jane were physically unharmed, the tragedy claimed Benjamin's life. Franklin discovered his son's decapitated body amid the wreckage and, in shock, covered him with his coat to shield Jane from the horrifying sight.

The loss shattered them both. Consumed by grief, Franklin became convinced that he was cursed by God, leading him to refuse the tradition of swearing on a Bible during his inauguration. His presidency was marked by deep sorrow and personal turmoil. He struggled with alcoholism, frequently drinking to the point of blacking out, while Jane retreated to the upstairs rooms of the White House, holding séances in a desperate attempt to reach their lost son.

Jane passed away ten years later, and Franklin succumbed to cirrhosis of the liver six years after her death, his life marked by profound tragedy and loss.

PETER THE NOT-SO-GREAT

Peter the Great, who ruled Russia from 1682 to 1725, is celebrated as one of the most influential leaders in Russian history. However, his legacy is also marked by deeply disturbing and cruel behavior that bordered on psychopathy.

Peter was plagued by an intense fear of monsters, leading him to command Russia's scientific community to study people with physical deformities, convinced that they might be real monsters. This obsession revealed his deep paranoia and callousness.

In 1717, Peter's mistress, Mary Hamilton, became pregnant. Fearing scandal, she used medication to hasten the birth and then killed the child, hoping to keep the secret from Peter. When he discovered her crime, he ordered her public execution by beheading. In a chilling display, Peter picked up her severed head, kissed it on the lips, and used it as a grotesque prop to lecture the shocked audience about human anatomy. He even kissed the head a second time before callously tossing it into the crowd.

Peter later married Catherine I, who eventually had an affair with a man named Peter le Monde. Upon discovering the infidelity, Peter had Catherine's lover executed and preserved his severed head in a jar. In a macabre twist, he forced his wife to keep the jar beside her bed, ensuring that she would "sleep next to her lover" every night.

Despite his remarkable achievements in modernizing Russia, Peter the Great's brutal actions and cruel eccentricities reveal a dark and complex side to his legacy.

THE WILD LIFE OF OLD HICKORY

Andrew Jackson, born on March 15, 1767, in the Carolinas, lived a life shaped by conflict and controversy from an early age. At just 14 years old, he was captured by British soldiers while acting as a courier for the colonial army during the American Revolution. When a British officer demanded that young Jackson polish his boots, he refused. In response, the officer struck him with a sword, leaving a deep gash on his head. This early encounter with violence set the tone for Jackson's turbulent life.

In his early adulthood, Jackson became involved in various ventures, including the controversial practice of slave trading. Operating between his home in Nashville, Tennessee, and Western Florida, he amassed considerable wealth as a slave owner, eventually holding a total of 300 enslaved people. Although Jackson saw himself as a benevolent master who treated his slaves with dignity, his actions painted a darker picture. He offered a cash reward for the capture of runaway slaves and imposed brutal punishments, including 300 lashes—often fatal—for those who were caught.

Jackson's views on race and his policies toward Native Americans were equally controversial. A staunch advocate for Indian removal, he disregarded existing treaties and pushed for the forced relocation of approximately 60,000 Native Americans to make way for white settlers. This policy culminated in the infamous Trail of Tears, a forced march that resulted in the deaths of thousands of Indigenous people.

Jackson's reputation for violence was further solidified in 1806 when he became embroiled in a dispute with Charles Dickinson over a horse race. After Dickinson refused to pay a forfeit fee, Jackson challenged him to a duel. He allowed Dickinson to shoot first, taking a bullet to the chest, but survived. Jackson then carefully aimed and fatally shot Dickinson. Over the course of his life, Jackson participated in more than 100 duels. By the time he became president, his body was riddled with bullets.

In 1835, while serving his second term as President of the United States, Jackson survived an assassination attempt when a man named Richard Lawrence tried to shoot him outside the Capitol. Both of Lawrence's guns misfired, and an enraged Jackson proceeded to beat the would-be assassin with his cane until Congressman Davy Crockett intervened. Lawrence, a mentally unstable house painter, believed he was King Richard II and that Jackson was preventing him from collecting money owed by the U.S. government.

After leaving office, Jackson remained a powerful figure in American politics, supporting Martin Van Buren's campaign and lobbying for the annexation of Texas. He passed away on June 8, 1845, from heart failure and tuberculosis. His funeral, however, was unexpectedly interrupted by his pet parrot, Poll, who had been taught a variety of swear words by Jackson. The bird's disruptive behavior led to its removal from the service, providing a final, quirky chapter to Jackson's tumultuous life.

CHAPTER 6

WHERE DID THAT COME FROM?

THE MOST-KISSED FACE ON EARTH

In the late 1800s, a mysterious body of a young woman was discovered floating in the River Seine in Paris, France. The young woman showed no signs of struggle, leading many to believe she had taken her own life. Despite efforts to identify her, no one came forward to claim the body or provide her name. She became known as L'Inconnue de la Seine—the Unknown Woman of the Seine—a haunting figure who would go on to achieve an unexpected kind of immortality.

After the discovery, her body was taken to the Paris morgue, where a pathologist was struck by the peculiar serenity of her face. Her expression, almost a faint smile, seemed out of place for someone who had met such a tragic end. Captivated by her peaceful demeanor, the pathologist created a plaster death mask of her face, preserving her features for posterity. What began as a scientific curiosity quickly became something far more profound.

The mask of L'Inconnue became a cultural phenomenon in Paris. Replicas were mass-produced, and it became morbidly fashionable to own or display her likeness.

Among the city's high society, the mask was often a centerpiece at parties—a reminder of beauty tinged with mystery and melancholy. Writers, artists, and intellectuals, including the philosopher Albert Camus, were drawn to her serene yet enigmatic expression.

As time passed, fascination with L'Inconnue extended far beyond France. Her image traveled across borders, captivating people throughout Europe and beyond.

Among those inspired was Åsmund Laerdal, a toymaker who, in the mid-20th century, sought a way to create a realistic mannequin for teaching cardiopulmonary resuscitation (CPR). Laerdal selected the mask of L'Inconnue for his invention, giving her face to Resusci Anne, the mannequin that would teach generations how to save lives and become the "most-kissed face of all time."

THE FASCIST AND THE FAD

In the 1960s and 1970s, Harold Von Braunhut became an active supporter of white supremacist groups, including the KKK and the Aryan Nations. Despite his Jewish heritage, he adopted the name "Von" to appear more German and distance himself from his background. In a startling turn of events, he began purchasing firearms for the KKK and secretly shipping them from his home.

Alongside his controversial political affiliations, Von Braunhut was a savvy businessman who built a lucrative mail-order empire. His first hit product was X-Ray Specs, novelty glasses that claimed to let wearers see through clothing. However, his most iconic creation was Sea Monkeys—packets of brine shrimp that seemed to spring to life when placed in water. Cleverly marketed as magical, pet-like creatures that children could raise at home, Sea Monkeys became one of the most beloved novelty toys of the 20th century.

Despite his success in the toy industry, Von Braunhut's troubling political ties cast a dark shadow over his legacy, revealing a complex and controversial figure behind some of America's most iconic childhood novelties.

SAFE SAX

Adolphe Sax, born Antoine-Joseph Sax in 1814 in present-day Belgium, led a life marked by an extraordinary series of near-death experiences. At just three years old, Sax drank what he thought was a bowl of milk, only to discover it was actually water laced with acid. Miraculously, he survived. On one occasion, young Adolphe fell from a third-story window, crashing onto a rock below, and was believed to have perished from the fall. Yet again, he defied the odds and survived. Another time, while walking along a riverbank, a piece of cobblestone fell from above, striking his head and knocking him unconscious and sending him falling into the river, where he nearly drowned. Later, he went to a room in his family's home to take a nap and almost died from inhaling fumes from still-wet furniture varnish.

These repeated brushes with death earned him the nickname "the ghost." No matter how many times he came close to perishing, Sax always emerged unscathed. He survived to adulthood, though his health remained fragile. In 1853, he was diagnosed with cancer, but once again, he defied the odds and recovered. However, pneumonia would eventually claim his life 40 years later.

Despite his remarkable ability to cheat death, Sax's life was marred by financial struggles. He declared bankruptcy three times, largely due to a series of costly patent lawsuits. By the time of his death in 1894, he had died penniless. The patent at the heart of these legal battles was for an instrument he had patented in 1846—one that bore his own name: the saxophone.

THE BIRTH OF THE PILL

After Samuel McCormick—son of inventor Cyrus McCormick—married Katherine in 1904, he began to show severe symptoms of schizophrenia. At that time, the condition was largely untreatable, and Katherine devoted herself to finding a way to help him.

Katherine, who had attended MIT and had aspirations of attending medical school before her marriage, believed that her husband's schizophrenia was linked to a defective adrenal gland that might be treatable with hormones. In her quest for medical expertise, she connected with Gregory Goodwin Pincus through her friend Margaret Sanger, the founder of Planned Parenthood.

Pincus had been working on a hormonal birth control pill but was struggling with a lack of funding. Although Katherine never found a cure for her husband's illness, she established a research foundation at Harvard Medical School to support hormonal research.

Ironically, the hormonal treatments she funded eventually led to the creation of the world's first birth control pill, which was released in 1957, revolutionizing reproductive health and women's rights.

WITCHY ORIGINS

In the 14th century, the bubonic plague, known as the Black Death, devastated England, killing about half of its population. While many at the time believed the plague was a punishment from God, it was actually spread by fleas carried on rats, which transmitted the disease to humans.

Single women who kept cats as pets were often spared from the worst of the plague. Their cats hunted the rats that carried the infected fleas, reducing their owners' chances of catching the disease. However, this led to suspicions that these women were protected by dark forces, causing them to be labeled as witches. This association eventually gave rise to the superstition linking witches to black cats.

The iconic image of witches flying on broomsticks is rooted in the practices of women accused of witchcraft. They would make a hallucinogenic ointment from nightshade and other herbs, which they applied to broomsticks. By rubbing the potion on the broom and then applying it to their bodies—particularly in areas that absorbed it quickly—they experienced intense hallucinations that gave them the sensation of flying.

This vivid, otherworldly experience contributed to the enduring myth of witches soaring through the skies on broomsticks.

FOR WHOM THE BELL TOLLS

Alexander Graham Bell, born in 1847 in Edinburgh, Scotland, grew up in a family devoted to language and communication. His mother, who began losing her hearing when he was 12, profoundly influenced his lifelong fascination with helping the hearing-impaired. Bell discovered that by pressing his mouth to her forehead and speaking clearly, vibrations from his voice could travel through the bones of her skull, allowing her to faintly hear. This experience sparked his enduring interest in acoustics and speech.

Bell's father, a scholar of elocution, further nurtured his curiosity. At 16, Bell and his brother built a life-sized model of the human vocal apparatus, complete with a larynx, skull, and mouth. The device produced sounds when air passed through it and the lips were adjusted. Bell's experiments extended to live subjects, including the family dog. By manipulating the dog's lips and throat while it growled, Bell managed to simulate speech, famously teaching it to "say" the phrase, "how are you, grandmama?"

In 1870, Bell moved to Canada and later to the United States, where he taught deaf students at various institutions. His innovative methods led him to open the School for Vocal Physiology and Mechanics of Speech in Boston. Among his students was Helen Keller, who credited Bell with opening the world of communication to her.

Bell's passion for sound culminated in the invention of the telephone. On March 7, 1876, he patented the device and made the first telephone call three days later, revolutionizing global communication.

The greeting "hello" became a standard thanks to Bell, although his colleague Thomas Edison had proposed "ahoy" instead. Through his groundbreaking work in sound and communication, Alexander Graham Bell transformed how people connected, leaving an enduring legacy in technological history.

THE BIRTH OF A MONSTER

In 1816, the eruption of Mount Tambora caused a drastic shift in the Earth's climate, resulting in a cooler, darker year known as The Year Without a Summer. As the world faced severe weather and agricultural failure, four young writers found themselves stuck in a Swiss home, unknowingly setting the stage for a revolution in horror literature.

Mary Wollstonecraft Godwin, born in 1797 in London, was the daughter of renowned feminist author Mary Wollstonecraft. In 1814, she began a relationship with Percy Shelley, a married man. Their secret romance led Mary Shelley to lose her virginity to Percy somewhere they knew they wouldn't get caught, atop her mother's grave. In Switzerland in May 1816, they joined the infamous poet Lord Byron. Byron, already infamous for his controversial affairs, including with Mary's stepsister, Claire Clairmont, hosted a summer gathering that would change literature forever.

Accompanied by Byron's personal physician, John Polidori, the group spent a dark, rainy summer together. One night, Lord Byron challenged everyone to see who could write the most terrifying story.

Polidori quickly produced The Vampyre, a tale of a blood-sucking monster based on Byron himself, becoming the first published novel featuring a vampire. The novel was released under Byron's name, though it was Polidori's work.

Meanwhile, Mary Shelley struggled with writer's block, until a vivid nightmare about a reanimated corpse inspired her. At just 19, she penned Frankenstein; or the Modern Prometheus, one of the most famous horror novels of all time, published in 1818.

Tragically, most of the summer's participants faced untimely deaths. Polidori committed suicide five years later, Percy Shelley drowned, and Byron died young. Mary Shelley lived to 53, her novel enduring for centuries.

CHAPTER 7

HISTORICAL TRUE CRIME

MOMMY DEAREST

In the early 1900s, Aurora Carballeira became deeply fascinated by eugenics—the idea of creating the perfect human being. After giving birth to her daughter, Hildegart, in 1914, Aurora embarked on an experiment to shape her child into this ideal person.

By the age of two, Hildegart was already reading, and by 10, she could speak four languages. At just 13, she enrolled in law school, and by 18, she became a professor at the same university. However, Aurora maintained total control over her daughter's life, suppressing her free thought and imposing her own ideals.

When H.G. Wells, the author of The War of the Worlds and The Time Machine, visited Madrid, he met Hildegart and was alarmed by her mother's overbearing influence. Concerned for Hildegart's well-being, Wells offered her a job as his secretary to help her escape her mother's control, but Aurora refused to let her go.

As Aurora's paranoia grew, she feared her daughter might try to break free from her grasp. In 1933, she entered Hildegart's room and shot her multiple times, killing her.

When questioned about the murder, Aurora chillingly explained, "When a sculptor finds an imperfection in their work, they destroy it."

WOW FACTOR

In 1926, gangster John Factor masterminded one of the largest stock frauds of his time, swindling $110 million in today's money from members of Britain's elite, including the British Royal Family. Following the scandal, Factor fled to Monaco and eventually settled in the United States to evade justice.

Despite his attempts to escape accountability, Factor was tried and convicted in the United States, receiving a 24-year prison sentence. In a bold and elaborate scheme to fight extradition, he allegedly staged the kidnapping of both himself and his son. The ruse proved successful, and Factor was released from prison, allowing him to remain in the United States.

Over time, Factor became deeply involved in U.S. politics, leveraging his wealth and connections to gain influence. His political ties reached their peak in 1962 when he faced deportation back to England. However, President John F. Kennedy intervened and halted the extradition. Notably, John Factor had been the largest individual donor to Kennedy's 1960 presidential campaign, raising questions about the motivations behind the president's decision.

Adding an intriguing twist to his story, John Factor was the younger brother of Max Factor, the legendary cosmetics entrepreneur whose name became synonymous with beauty and glamour. While Max Factor revolutionized the cosmetics industry, John Factor carved a legacy of infamy, weaving his way through crime, scandal, and politics.

SCOT-FREE

Gregor MacGregor was a Scottish soldier from a distinguished family, descending from the notorious outlaw Rob Roy. Renowned for his bravery and leadership, MacGregor earned high honors in the Scottish military.

In 1838, he moved to Venezuela, where he married a cousin of the revolutionary leader Simón Bolívar and joined the struggle for the country's independence. Despite his valor on the battlefield, MacGregor was secretly embezzling large sums from the Venezuelan government. When his schemes were at risk of being uncovered, he fled to Honduras unscathed.

While in Honduras, MacGregor concocted an elaborate hoax. He wrote letters to his contacts in Scotland, claiming he had been granted the title of "Cazique" (chief) of a nation called "Poyais." Returning to London with forged documents, including the so-called Constitution of Poyais, he portrayed this fictional land as a paradise brimming with opportunity. His convincing tales persuaded the British government to invest heavily in the development of Poyais.

MacGregor then led hundreds of hopeful British settlers to Honduras, promising them land and prosperity. Upon arrival, they were horrified to find no civilization, only uninhabitable jungle. Stranded and unprepared, 150 settlers perished from starvation and disease.

Despite orchestrating one of history's greatest frauds, causing mass suffering, and stealing millions from the British government, MacGregor faced no legal consequences. He eventually returned to Venezuela with his wealth intact. In 1845, he died in Caracas at the age of 58 and was buried with full military honors, leaving behind a legacy of deception and tragedy.

NESS' MONSTER

From 1934 to 1938, Cleveland, Ohio, was terrorized by a series of grisly murders attributed to the Cleveland Torso Murderer. Over a dozen dismembered bodies were discovered, mostly in impoverished areas known as Hoovervilles—makeshift communities named after President Herbert Hoover during the Great Depression. The killer targeted poor residents, decapitating them and cutting their bodies in half. Many of the remains went undiscovered for years.

At the height of the killings, Cleveland's Public Safety Director, Eliot Ness—best known for leading the Untouchables in bringing down Al Capone—launched an intense investigation. In an effort to clear out the areas where the murders occurred, Ness resorted to drastic measures, ordering the burning of the Hoovervilles. Despite his efforts, the killer remained elusive.

Ness's investigation eventually led to a primary suspect: Dr. Francis Sweeney, a local physician. After intense interrogation, Ness believed he was close to solving the case. However, the killer taunted him by leaving two more dismembered bodies in the grass outside his office.

This chilling act further cemented the murderer's ability to evade capture, and the Cleveland Torso Murderer was never brought to justice.

To this day, the true identity of the killer remains a mystery, marking one of the most disturbing unsolved crime sprees in American history.

SLAVE GEORGE

In the early 1800s, Charles and Lucy Lewis were slave owners, with George, a young man, among their enslaved. Charles was the cousin of Merryweather Lewis, famed for the Lewis and Clark expedition commissioned by President Thomas Jefferson. When Lucy passed away in 1810, George, then 17, was transferred to Charles' son, Lilburn. Tragically, on December 15th, 1811, a minor accident occurred: George inadvertently broke a cherished glass pitcher that had belonged to Lilburn's late mother.

Enraged by this mishap, Lilburn and his brother Isham responded with brutal violence. They tied George to the floor and mercilessly decapitated him with an axe. To conceal their crime, they coerced other enslaved individuals to dismember George's body and burn the remains in a fireplace. However, a violent earthquake struck that very night, destroying the fireplace and thwarting their attempt to dispose of the evidence.

News of the atrocity spread rapidly, largely due to the brothers' connections: their deceased mother, Lucy Jefferson-Lewis, had been the sister of President Thomas Jefferson. Despite being arrested for murder,

Lilburn and Isham were swiftly released on bail, underscoring the privilege that shielded them from immediate consequences. The case garnered widespread attention, exposing the stark realities of violence and impunity within the system of slavery, even among families connected to the highest echelons of American society.

BERT AND ERNIE

Robert St. John was a journalist for the Chicago Daily News in the early 1920s, where he began the dangerous task of investigating the infamous gangster Al Capone. He wrote a series of exposés that brought attention to Capone's criminal empire. However, shortly after these articles were published, Capone's men tracked down St. John and brutally beat him within an inch of his life.

After the attack, St. John went to the police, who arranged a face-to-face meeting with Capone himself. During the meeting, Capone offered St. John money to stay silent, but St. John refused the bribe. Despite the attack, he didn't back down. He quit his job at the Daily News and moved on to write for the Associated Press, where he covered Franklin Roosevelt's presidential campaign.

Though St. John's career was remarkable, his journey to success wasn't without discouragement. In high school, his teacher told him and a classmate to give up on their dreams of becoming writers, claiming they would never learn how to write.

Both St. John and his classmate, Ernest Hemingway, ignored the teacher's words and went on to achieve greatness in the world of journalism and literature.

A FLINGA WITH INGA

Inga Arvad was born in Denmark in 1913 and won the title of Miss Denmark in 1931 before embarking on a career in journalism. During her time as a journalist, she crossed paths with Adolf Hitler, who became notably infatuated with her. In fact, she attended the 1936 Berlin Olympics as Hitler's "date," further cementing her connection to the Nazi leader.

Shortly afterward, the Nazis approached Inga with an offer to become a spy for Germany. Although she initially considered the proposition, fear compelled her to flee the country.

By 1941, Inga had relocated to the United States, where she began a passionate affair with a young man that soon caught the attention of the FBI. Suspecting that she was a Nazi spy, J. Edgar Hoover became convinced that Inga was using her charm and beauty to infiltrate high-level circles within the U.S. government.

The young man at the center of this scandal turned out to be the 24-year-old son of former U.S. Ambassador to England and Nazi sympathizer Joseph Kennedy.

That 24-year-old son was future President of the United States John F. Kennedy.

SICKLES' "L"

Daniel Sickles was a New York congressman whose political career was marred by scandal when it was revealed that he was having an affair with a well-known prostitute named Fanny White. Rumors swirled that Sickles even engaged in the affair within the chambers of the New York State Assembly, leading to his expulsion from the Assembly.

Years earlier, while on a political trip to London, Sickles met Queen Victoria. In an audacious move, he introduced her to his "wife." In truth, his actual wife, Teresa, was back home in New York, pregnant. The woman he presented as his spouse was none other than Fanny White, his mistress.

Upon returning from London, Sickles discovered that his wife, Teresa, had been having an affair. Consumed with rage, he confronted her lover, Philip Barton Key, right across the street from the White House. Key was the son of Francis Scott Key, the man who wrote The Star-Spangled Banner. In a fit of jealousy and anger, Sickles shot Key dead in broad daylight.

During his trial, Sickles employed a groundbreaking legal defense. His lawyers—one of whom was Edwin Stanton, who would later serve as Abraham Lincoln's Secretary of War—argued that Sickles had acted under temporary insanity. This was the first time in U.S. legal history that the temporary insanity defense was used. The strategy proved successful, and Sickles was acquitted of murder.

Daniel Sickles' life was marked by scandal, political intrigue, and legal precedent, securing his place as one of the most controversial figures in American history.

GRANDPA GETTY

J. Paul Getty, the founder of Getty Oil Company, was the wealthiest private citizen in the world during the 1960s. In 1973, his 16-year-old grandson, John Paul Getty III, was kidnapped while in Rome. The abductors, fully aware of the family's vast fortune, demanded a $17 million ransom for his safe release.

Desperate to save his son, Getty's son reached out to his father for help. However, J. Paul Getty refused, arguing that paying the ransom would encourage future kidnappings. In a horrifying turn of events, the kidnappers sent an envelope containing John Paul's severed ear, along with a reduced ransom demand of $3.2 million.

Faced with this gruesome proof, J. Paul Getty finally agreed to pay $2.2 million—the maximum amount that was tax-deductible. He then loaned his son the remaining $1 million at 4% interest. On December 15, 1973, John Paul Getty III was found alive at a gas station shortly after the ransom was paid.

Despite the ordeal, when the rescued teenager called his grandfather to thank him, Getty refused to take the call, maintaining his distant and cold demeanor even after his grandson's harrowing experience.

A STRANGE REQUEST

Peter Kürten is remembered as one of the most terrifying criminals in history. His violent tendencies emerged at an alarmingly young age—at just five years old, he tried to drown a playmate. As he grew older, his depravity deepened, leading him to engage in bestiality, during which he admitted to killing the animals at the moment of climax. His violent urges escalated to human victims, and in 1931, he was arrested for the brutal murders of nine people and the attempted murders of seven others, many of whom were children under the age of 14.

Before his execution by beheading, Kürten asked the prison psychiatrist a chilling question: "After my head is chopped off, will I still be able to hear, at least for a moment, the sound of my own blood gushing from the stump of my neck? That would be the pleasure to end all pleasures." This haunting statement revealed his profound obsession with violence and death.

Kürten's gruesome crimes partly inspired the character of the serial killer in Fritz Lang's 1931 film M, masterfully portrayed by Peter Lorre.

In a strange twist of fate, Lorre's daughter narrowly escaped becoming a victim of the Hillside Stranglers, a pair of notorious serial killers, because they recognized who her father was and let her go.

Peter Kürten's story remains one of the darkest chapters in criminal history, influencing cinema and chilling audiences long after his death.

Historical True Crime

FRANK'S MURDER HOUSE

While famed architect Frank Lloyd Wright was away on a business trip, his mistress hosted a gathering at their home, Taliesin. During the event, one of the caretakers, Julian Carlton, approached her and mentioned that the rugs looked dirty, offering to take them outside for cleaning.

But instead of carrying out this task, Carlton went outside and began nailing shut every window of the historic house with chilling precision. Once his grim preparations were complete, he set the entire building on fire. As the flames engulfed Taliesin, two children who were sitting on the porch became his first victims when Carlton approached them with an axe and brutally killed them.

Inside, guests desperately shattered windows to escape the raging blaze. But Carlton was waiting outside, axe in hand, ready to attack those who fled. His rampage resulted in seven deaths and multiple injuries before he was finally apprehended. Carlton was sentenced to life in prison, where he eventually starved himself to death, taking the reason for his horrific actions to his grave.

CHAPTER 8

SCIENCE GONE WRONG

A LITTLE OFF THE TOP

The transorbital lobotomy—an invasive procedure involving the insertion of an ice pick-like instrument through the eye socket into the brain—was once widely regarded as a revolutionary treatment for mental illness, despite its brutal nature. This controversial procedure was popularized by Dr. Walter Freeman, who began performing lobotomies in 1936. Over the next few decades, Freeman conducted more than 4,000 lobotomies, with over 100 patients dying as a direct result.

Known for his flamboyant showmanship, Freeman often held public demonstrations to showcase his speed and skill in performing lobotomies. In some instances, he operated on two patients at once, simultaneously wielding an ice pick in each hand.

One of Freeman's most notorious patients was Rosemary Kennedy, daughter of Joseph Kennedy and sister of future President John F. Kennedy. Concerned by Rosemary's erratic behavior and fearing she did not live up to the family's expectations, her father authorized the lobotomy.

During the operation, Freeman instructed her to recite "The Lord's Prayer" and "God Bless America" repeatedly. He continued the procedure until she could no longer remember the words, having severely damaged her frontal lobe. As a result, Rosemary was left in a vegetative state for the remainder of her life.

In 1951, while performing a lobotomy on another female patient, Freeman turned to pose for a photograph, not realizing that his hand holding the ice pick was still moving.

The instrument penetrated too deeply into the patient's brain, killing her instantly in front of a horrified audience.

Though once hailed as a pioneering figure, Freeman's brutal methods and reckless disregard for patient safety eventually led to his professional downfall. Today, his practices serve as a grim reminder of the dark history of psychiatric treatment.

CAVITY COTTON

Dr. Henry Cotton, born on May 18, 1876, in Norfolk, Virginia, was a prominent yet controversial figure in early 20th-century psychiatry. After studying medicine at Johns Hopkins University, Cotton traveled to Europe in 1906 to study under Alois Alzheimer, whose research on dementia profoundly influenced his career. This training solidified Cotton's interest in understanding the causes of mental illness, ultimately leading him to embrace a radical and deeply flawed medical theory.

At the time, some psychiatrists believed that mental disorders could result from infections. Inspired by the discovery that syphilis could cause psychosis in its advanced stages, Cotton hypothesized that dental decay was a primary source of such infections. As superintendent of the New Jersey State Hospital, he began extracting the teeth of mentally ill patients in an attempt to cure their conditions. When tooth extractions failed to yield consistent results, Cotton escalated his interventions, performing tonsillectomies.

Still unsatisfied, he expanded his efforts to even more invasive procedures, removing organs such as the gallbladder, spleen, testicles, ovaries, and parts of the colon—believing these surgeries could eliminate hidden infections and, in turn, mental illness.

Cotton claimed an astounding success rate of 85%, earning international recognition. Prestigious outlets like The New York Times praised his work, and he was hailed as a pioneer in psychiatry. However, closer scrutiny revealed serious flaws. His records were poorly maintained, and independent reviews debunked his claims of success. Worse still, his treatments carried a shockingly high mortality rate of 45%, with many patients dying from surgical complications.

Despite mounting criticism, Cotton avoided significant professional consequences. He retired in 1930 as medical director emeritus, and some of his less extreme procedures persisted in medical practice until the 1950s. Cotton died in 1933, leaving behind a legacy marked by both misguided innovation and profound tragedy.

HOLMESBURG HORRORS

In the early 1950s, dermatologist Dr. Albert Kligman conducted a series of brutal experiments on inmates at Holmesburg Prison in Philadelphia, Pennsylvania—a facility grimly known as "The Terrordome." Funded by Johnson & Johnson and the U.S. Army, these experiments aimed to test the effectiveness of various medications for treating skin damage.

To carry out his research, Dr. Kligman intentionally inflicted severe skin damage on the inmates. In some tests, he applied acid directly to their testicles, causing excruciating blistering. In one of the most grotesque procedures, he sewed cadaver tissue onto the backs of living inmates to see if the dead tissue could be revived and function normally.

An estimated 85 percent of the prisoners at Holmesburg were used as unwilling test subjects in these experiments. The testing continued until 1974, when a series of class-action lawsuits finally brought the unethical practices to an end.

TWAIN'S ACCIDENT

When Nikola Tesla was living in Croatia, he fell seriously ill and found solace in the works of Mark Twain, whose books brought him comfort during his recovery. Years later, after moving to the United States, Tesla was eager to meet the author who had unknowingly helped him through such a difficult time. Twenty-five years after they first exchanged letters, Tesla and Twain finally met and quickly formed a close friendship. Twain became a frequent visitor to Tesla's laboratory, fascinated by his inventions and experiments.

On one particular visit, Twain mentioned that he was suffering from severe constipation. Tesla, ever the inventor, suggested that Twain try out a vibrating platform he had recently developed, believing it would stimulate his digestive system and relieve his discomfort. Twain stepped onto the machine and, enjoying the tingling sensation, insisted on staying on longer than Tesla recommended.

However, after a few minutes, Twain's face changed as the device worked a little too effectively. In a moment of panic, he urgently asked Tesla to stop the machine, having unexpectedly lost control of his bowels. The two men shared an awkward but memorable moment, adding a humorous chapter to their remarkable friendship.

TEWKSBURY TERROR

Tewksbury State Hospital, an institution in Massachusetts established to assist impoverished children, harbored some of the most horrifying abuses in American history. Initially presented as a charitable facility, its dark reality was exposed in 1875 when reports revealed shocking atrocities occurring within its walls.

To generate revenue, the hospital's administrators starved infants to death and sold their bodies to medical institutions for $3 each, a practice that claimed the lives of approximately 200 infants annually. Adults were not spared from cruelty either; some were killed, and their skin was reportedly used to produce leather goods for profit. The facility's conditions were appalling, with patients suffering unimaginable neglect. There were even accounts of rats chewing holes in patients' scalps as they lay helpless at night.

The horrifying abuses at Tewksbury persisted until 1883, when a committee hearing finally brought them to light, leading to widespread outrage and the eventual reform of the institution. Among the survivors of this grim chapter was a young girl named Anne Sullivan.

Despite enduring severe hardships at Tewksbury, Sullivan overcame her traumatic past to achieve remarkable success. She later became renowned as the teacher of Helen Keller, famously known as the Miracle Worker, leaving a legacy of resilience and hope that contrasted sharply with the horrors she endured in her youth.

THE CURSED CURE

John Taylor was an English occultist in the 1700s who claimed to have discovered a cure for cataracts. Traveling across Europe in a stagecoach decorated with painted eyeballs, he performed eye surgeries as part of a traveling medicine show. After conducting his procedures and collecting payment, Taylor would swiftly leave town.

His quick exits were not just a matter of routine—they were a cover for his fraudulent practices. Taylor's "cure" involved dripping a concoction of pigeon blood and salt into his patients' eyes. Far from healing them, this mixture worsened their vision and often led to complete blindness. By the time his victims realized they had been duped, Taylor was long gone, moving on to his next unsuspecting town.

Over his career, Taylor is believed to have blinded more than 100 people, including notable figures like composer Johann Sebastian Bach and George Handel. Tragically, both men died from infections caused by Taylor's so-called eye surgeries, cementing his legacy as one of history's most infamous medical frauds.

EVIL EXPIREMENTS OF UNIT 731

During World War II, the Japanese military created a secret research unit known as Unit 731 under their Biological Chemical Research Division. Its purpose was to carry out brutal experiments on live human subjects, eerily similar to the atrocities committed by Nazi doctor Josef Mengele. Most of these experiments were conducted on Chinese prisoners.

One particularly horrific experiment involved the intentional spread of sexually transmitted diseases. Thousands of Chinese prisoners were deliberately infected with gonorrhea and syphilis as part of gruesome medical studies. Yet, this was only the beginning of the unit's inhumane activities.

In another disturbing procedure, prisoners had their limbs amputated—either an arm or a leg—to observe how long it would take for them to bleed to death. Others were subjected to a giant centrifuge, spun at high speeds until they died from the extreme forces.

These experiments were not isolated incidents; they were systematically performed on an estimated 200,000 to 300,000 human beings. Unit 731's actions represent one of the darkest chapters of human experimentation in history, reflecting the horrifying extent of wartime cruelty.

HEIMLICH'S MANEUVER

In 1993, Joanne Carson, the ex-wife of Tonight Show host Johnny Carson, hosted a gathering at her home featuring a lecture by Dr. Henry Heimlich, the inventor of the Heimlich maneuver. Heimlich claimed to have found a cure for AIDS by injecting HIV-positive patients with malaria.

The event was attended by a star-studded audience, including Jack Nicholson, Bob Hope, Jon Voight, and Ron Howard. Enthralled by Heimlich's bold claims, the celebrities donated a total of $600,000 to fund his controversial research. Heimlich planned to use this money to travel to China, where he intended to inject HIV-positive patients with malaria, believing that the malaria infection would stimulate an immune response capable of fighting HIV.

However, his theory lacked any scientific backing and was widely criticized by the US Centers for Disease Control and the medical community. Even his own son, Peter Heimlich, publicly condemned his father's dangerous experiments. After facing intense public backlash and the deaths of several patients, Dr. Heimlich eventually abandoned his controversial research.

RADIUM GIRLS

From 1917 to the mid-1920s, the United States Radium Corporation produced glowing watch dials for military personnel by painting them with radium, a highly toxic substance. The women working in the factory were instructed to use their lips to shape the paintbrush tips for precision, unknowingly ingesting large amounts of radium in the process.

As time passed, the women began to experience alarming health issues. They lost their teeth, developed ulcers, and suffered from severe lesions. One worker even had her lower jaw removed due to jaw necrosis, a direct result of the radiation exposure. Despite the clear signs of radiation poisoning, the corporation falsely claimed that she had contracted syphilis, insisting the radium had no connection to her illness.

Most of the women suffered various health problems, and over 30 died from radiation-related illnesses. Despite the obvious dangers, the company did not take responsibility for the harm caused. It wasn't until the Radium Dial case went to court that justice was pursued, but it took eight trials before the workers were finally compensated for their suffering.

The tragic legacy of these women helped to raise awareness about workplace safety and the dangers of radiation exposure, marking a pivotal moment in labor rights history.

THE WORLD'S MOST TOXIC MAN

While scientists were working on the Manhattan Project to create the first atomic bomb, they needed to handle large amounts of a radioactive element called plutonium. To better understand the long-term effects of plutonium exposure, they collaborated with a team of doctors to conduct experiments on human test subjects.

They decided that the most ethical and humane approach was to find patients diagnosed with terminal cancer and tell them they would receive experimental cancer treatment. One such patient was an Ohio man named Albert Stevens. Stevens had recently been experiencing severe stomach pains and finally sought medical attention. His doctor diagnosed him with stomach cancer, claiming it was terminal.

Stevens then became patient CAL-1 in the plutonium radiation experiments. On May 14, 1945, he received an injection of plutonium without ever being informed of its true nature. His dose was the largest amount of plutonium ever administered to a single human—60 times the maximum radiation exposure allowed for U.S. radiation workers.

After the experiment, Stevens returned to the hospital for cancer surgery. However, when surgeons analyzed the mass they had removed, they were shocked to discover that it was not a tumor but a gastric ulcer. Albert Stevens had never had cancer. His initial diagnosis had been incorrect, leading him to receive a potentially lethal dose of plutonium that he never should have been exposed to.

Stevens was never informed of his misdiagnosis and lived the rest of his life believing that his "cancer" had been completely treated.

CHAPTER 9

CLOSE CALLS AND STRANGE DEATHS

THE WILD DEATH OF A FOUNDING FATHER

Gouverneur Morris, one of the founding fathers of the United States, was born in the Bronx, New York, in 1752. He became an influential member of the Continental Congress and served as a spokesman for the Continental Army, working closely with General George Washington. In 1778, Morris signed the Articles of Confederation, solidifying his place in American history. Shortly after, he lost his left leg in an accident and wore a peg leg for the rest of his life. Later, he served as a New York senator and played a key role in designing the Manhattan street grid.

Morris eventually married Anne Richardson, whose past was shrouded in scandal. Before their marriage, Anne was rumored to have had an affair with her sister's husband, resulting in a pregnancy. To avoid public disgrace, she and her sister's husband allegedly killed the baby. Despite knowing about this dark chapter, Gouverneur Morris chose to marry her.

In 1816, Morris suffered from a urinary tract blockage. In a desperate attempt to relieve the obstruction, he inserted a piece of whale bone into his urethra.

The improvised procedure led to a severe infection, and Morris died from the complications in November of that year.

A TANGLED TALE

Thomas Midgley rose to prominence for developing ethyl for gasoline, a compound that relied heavily on toxic lead. Despite clear evidence of its dangers, Midgley insisted it was safe. However, factory workers exposed to ethyl began experiencing severe hallucinations, and at least ten people died due to lead poisoning. In a dramatic attempt to prove its safety, Midgley poured ethyl over his body and inhaled its vapors for over a minute, a stunt that left him severely poisoned by lead.

After leaving the gasoline industry, Midgley turned his attention to refrigeration and developed Freon, a chlorofluorocarbon later discovered to be highly toxic and damaging to the ozone layer. His role in popularizing both ethyl and Freon has led many to claim that he caused more environmental harm than any other individual in history.

In his 50s, Midgley contracted polio, which left him partially paralyzed. To regain some independence, he designed a complex system of pulleys and ropes to help him get in and out of bed.

Tragically, in 1940, at the age of 53, he became entangled in the ropes and accidentally strangled himself.

Midgley's legacy is a paradox of brilliance and disaster—his inventions revolutionized industry but also caused catastrophic environmental and health consequences that persist to this day.

A FROZEN HELL

Antarctica, a land of extremes, has tested the limits of human endurance for centuries. Its hostile environment, with temperatures plunging to -128.6°F and winds exceeding 120 mph, makes it one of the most uninhabitable places on Earth. Yet early explorers braved its dangers to uncover its mysteries.

In 1907, Ernest Shackleton's Nimrod Expedition made history by summiting Mount Erebus, an active volcano, and reaching the South Magnetic Pole. Among Shackleton's team was Douglas Mawson, a young scientist destined to lead his own Antarctic odyssey.

In 1912, Mawson returned as the leader of the Australasian Antarctic Expedition. Facing some of the harshest conditions on record, Mawson and his team battled winds of up to 200 mph while charting the continent's icy expanse. In November, Mawson, Xavier Mertz, and Belgrave Ninnis embarked on a sled journey to map uncharted territory. Tragedy struck when Ninnis fell into the depths of a crevasse, taking vital supplies and sled dogs with him.

Left with only a week's rations, Mawson and Mertz began their grueling 300-mile return to base. To survive, they resorted to eating their remaining dogs—an act that likely caused hypervitaminosis A due to consuming the dogs' livers. The condition led to severe frostbite, delirium, and physical deterioration. Mertz succumbed to his suffering on December 8, leaving Mawson to complete the final 100 miles alone.

Battling the elements and his failing body, Mawson narrowly survived a fall into a crevasse and endured the agony of his skin peeling away from his frostbitten feet. Miraculously, he reached safety, though severely malnourished and near death.

After recovering, Mawson returned to Australia, served in World War I, and later became a respected geology professor. His resilience and determination solidified his legacy as one of Antarctica's greatest explorers.

THE FIRST DETECTIVE

Allan Pinkerton, born on August 21, 1819, in Glasgow, Scotland, immigrated to the United States in 1842 and settled in Dundee, Illinois. A former cooper, Pinkerton became involved with abolitionists near Chicago, turning his home into a stop on the Underground Railroad. His father's work as a police officer influenced his interest in detective work, and in 1844, he made his first mark by helping to capture a gang of counterfeiters hiding in the woods near his home.

By 1849, he became Chicago's first official detective, and a year later, he founded the Pinkerton National Detective Agency. Pinkerton's agency quickly gained prominence, particularly for its efforts in combating train robberies for railroad companies. During this time, he developed a relationship with an attorney for the Illinois Central Railroad named Abraham Lincoln (yes, that Abraham Lincoln). Pinkerton's abolitionist values led him to support John Brown's 1859 raid on Harpers Ferry, even purchasing the suit Brown would later wear during his execution.

With the onset of the Civil War in 1861, Pinkerton's agency was tasked with protecting the now President Abraham Lincoln and successfully prevented several assassination attempts. Despite their efforts, Lincoln was assassinated in 1865. During the war, Pinkerton's detectives also went undercover to gather intelligence for Union commanders.

After the war, the agency resumed its focus on pursuing train robbers, including Jesse James and his gang, though Pinkerton ultimately failed to capture them.

In 1884, Allan Pinkerton suffered a fatal accident when he slipped and bit his tongue, leading to a gangrene infection. He passed away on July 1, 1885.

While Pinkerton's work left a lasting impact on U.S. law enforcement, his agency's later actions tarnished his legacy. The Pinkerton Agency became notorious for suppressing labor movements on behalf of business leaders. Its most infamous role was during the Homestead Strike of 1892, when Pinkerton agents, hired by Andrew Carnegie's steel company, clashed with striking workers in Pittsburgh, Pennsylvania. The confrontation left 16 people dead, solidifying the agency's controversial reputation.

GOING OUT WITH A BANG

William the Conqueror, born in 1028, became the first Norman King of England after leading his forces to victory at the Battle of Hastings in 1066. His reign had a profound impact on English history, but he was also known for his considerable weight.

In 1087, while riding his horse, the pommel of his saddle pressed painfully into his abdomen, rupturing his intestines and leading to a severe infection that ultimately proved fatal. Due to his large size, William's body could not fit in a standard stone coffin, so it was left exposed during his funeral.

According to historical accounts, the infection in his intestines caused an extreme buildup of gas. When attendants tried to squeeze his body into the custom-made coffin, his abdomen burst, releasing a foul odor and scattering bodily fluids among the horrified mourners.

This gruesome incident added a macabre twist to the end of William's influential life, leaving behind a legacy marked by both conquest and a rather explosive final farewell.

DEATH OF A DAREDEVIL

Bobby Leach, born in Lancaster, England, in 1858, was a daring performer with the Barnum and Bailey Circus, renowned for his expertise in executing dangerous stunts. His thrill-seeking nature made him a natural fit for feats that most would consider unthinkable.

On October 24, 1901, Leach learned of an extraordinary achievement that captured global attention. Annie Taylor, a 63-year-old woman, had become the first person to survive a descent over Niagara Falls in a barrel. Inspired by her daring, Leach set his sights on accomplishing the same feat.

Nearly a decade later, on July 25, 1911, Bobby Leach became the second person to conquer Niagara Falls in a barrel. However, the stunt came at a significant cost. Leach sustained severe injuries, including two broken kneecaps and a fractured jaw, which required a six-month hospital stay to recover. Despite the physical toll, the feat elevated Leach to celebrity status, cementing his reputation as a fearless daredevil.

Tragically, it was an entirely different kind of fall that would seal Leach's fate. In 1926, while on a publicity tour in New Zealand, Leach slipped on an orange peel, injuring his leg. The seemingly minor incident took a dire turn when the wound became severely infected, leading to gangrene. Despite the amputation of his leg in an effort to save his life, Leach succumbed to complications from the infection two months later.

Bobby Leach's life was a paradox of daring triumphs and unforeseen tragedy. From his high-risk stunts to his ironic and untimely demise, his story remains a testament to the unpredictable nature of a life lived on the edge.

DEATHS IN THE DYNASTY

The Rockefeller name is synonymous with wealth, power, and influence in the United States, often linked to conspiracy theories and secret societies like the Illuminati. This iconic family's legacy began with John D. Rockefeller, born in 1839 to a modest family. After working from a young age to support his parents, John entered the early oil industry and founded Standard Oil in 1870. By 1900, Standard Oil controlled 90% of U.S. oil production. The company was broken up in 1911 due to antitrust laws, giving rise to major companies like ExxonMobil and Chevron.

By 1913, Rockefeller's wealth had reached nearly $30 billion in today's money. He devoted the rest of his life to philanthropy, funding medical and educational initiatives, including founding the University of Chicago. He passed away in 1937 at age 97. His descendants continued to make their mark in unique ways. Nelson Rockefeller, his grandson, served as the Governor of New York from 1959 to 1973 and was an advocate for civil rights. He also served as Vice President under Gerald Ford after Nixon's resignation in 1974.

However, his life ended tragically in 1979 after suffering a heart attack during an affair with 25-year-old Megan Marshack, raising questions about the circumstances.

Michael Rockefeller, Nelson's son and John D.'s great-grandson, also led an adventurous life. In 1961, while on an expedition in Dutch New Guinea, he disappeared after a canoe accident.

Despite theories of shark attacks or drowning, some believe he was killed and possibly cannibalized by the local Asmat tribe. His disappearance remains unsolved, adding a chilling chapter to the Rockefeller family saga.

GOODNIGHT, MARGARET

Margaret Wise Brown, born on May 23, 1910, in Brooklyn, New York, came from a family with a notable legacy. Her grandfather, Benjamin Gratz Brown, had been the governor of Missouri and a Democratic vice-presidential candidate in 1872, though he lost to Ulysses S. Grant. Brown was passionate about writing from a young age, and after earning an English degree in 1932, she began teaching at the Bank Street Experimental School in New York.

In 1937, she published her first book, When the Wind Blew, and soon after became an editor at Harper & Brothers. There, she helped launch the career of fellow writer Gertrude Stein. In 1942, she wrote The Runaway Bunny, followed by the beloved classic Goodnight Moon in 1947. Although Goodnight Moon is now considered a children's literary masterpiece, it initially sold poorly, with only 6,000 copies sold at first.

Interestingly, Brown didn't particularly like children, admitting she didn't enjoy them "as a group." However, she embraced a childlike whimsy, spending her first royalty check on flowers and once getting into trouble in France for bringing an orange tree and live birds into a hotel room.

In 1952, Brown became engaged to James Rockefeller Jr., but her life was tragically cut short. While in France, she suffered a ruptured appendix and, after surgery, kicked her leg in the air to show the nurses how well she was recovering, unknowingly dislodging a blood clot that caused a fatal embolism.

Margaret Wise Brown died at 42, but her legacy endures through the millions of copies sold of Goodnight Moon.

IT'S MY PARTY, AND I'LL DIE IF I WANT TO

In 1846, a group of families from Springfield, Illinois, set out on a journey to the western United States, hoping to settle in California. Led by George Donner, the group, which eventually numbered nearly 90 people, became infamous as the Donner Party after a tragic series of events. While attempting a supposed shortcut through the Sierra Nevada mountains, they were trapped by heavy snowfall.

The worsening conditions left the Donner Party stranded for nearly four months. Their provisions dwindled rapidly, and starvation loomed over the group during the brutal winter months. Facing certain death, a group of 15 members—10 men and 5 women—ventured out to find help. Eight of the men perished during the journey, and the survivors resorted to cannibalism, consuming the bodies of the deceased to stay alive. This desperate group eventually reached California and organized a rescue mission. The first rescue effort brought 23 survivors to safety.

Back in the mountains, the remaining members endured unimaginable hardship, resorting to cannibalism to survive until further rescue missions could reach them. Of the original 87 members of the Donner Party, only 48 survived the ordeal.

The tragedy was rooted in a fateful decision to follow a supposed shortcut, which was claimed to save 300 miles of travel. The route, proposed by James F. Reed, a Springfield businessman, proved disastrous. Before the full extent of their plight was realized, the group banished Reed for other reasons, sparing him from the horrors to come.

Ironically, Reed's Springfield connections might have altered history itself. He had invited his friend, a young attorney named Abraham Lincoln, to join the expedition. Lincoln considered the offer but ultimately stayed behind, persuaded by his wife Mary Todd not to leave her and their growing family. This twist of fate spared the future 16th president from sharing in the Donner Party's tragic fate.

CHAPTER 10

ODDITIES

THE WORLD'S GREATEST SHOWMAN?

Phineas Taylor Barnum was born on July 5, 1810, in Bethel, Connecticut. He became famous for founding Barnum's American Museum in Manhattan in 1841, which quickly gained attention for its live oddities. Barnum's early exhibitions included showcasing albino people, dwarfs, and magicians. He was also notorious for presenting hoaxes, the first being the "Feejee mermaid," which was simply the body of a monkey sewn to the tail of a fish.

In 1835, P.T. Barnum began his career by exploiting a woman named Joice Heth, who his friend claimed was the former nanny of President George Washington. Barnum leased Heth for a year, showcasing her as a 161-year-old woman. To make her seem older, Barnum force-fed her whiskey and had her teeth removed. Barnum exhibited her for nearly 12 hours a day, earning the equivalent of $43,000 a week while Heth received none of the profits. After her death, Barnum hosted a public autopsy, revealing Heth was only 80 years old, further demonstrating his lack of morality and growing exploitation.

Barnum's most famous attraction was Charles Stratton, a five-year-old dwarf whom Barnum renamed General Tom Thumb. Barnum trained Stratton to sing, dance, and perform comedy acts, taking him on a successful European tour and even introducing him to Queen Victoria. Stratton's performances made a lasting impact, changing public perception of freak shows. His popularity also led to an invitation to the White House from President Abraham Lincoln to celebrate his marriage to Lavinia Wright.

In the first five years, Barnum's museum attracted nearly half a million visitors annually. It later became home to America's first aquarium, which housed beluga whales that often died quickly. When the museum burned down in 1865, two whales perished in the fire. Other curiosities Barnum featured included conjoined twins Chang and Eng, a man named Zip the Pinhead, and a woman with four legs.

At 60, Barnum transitioned to a traveling circus, eventually merging with James Bailey to create "Barnum and Bailey's Circus." He bought his most famous attraction, Jumbo the elephant, and popularized the term "jumbo" for anything large. Barnum's legacy continued until his death from a stroke on April 7, 1891, at the age of 80.

BLOODY MARY

Mary Toft was born in 1703 in Surrey, England, and in 1726, she became pregnant with her fourth child. However, her pregnancy took a strange turn when she began expelling animal parts instead of human flesh. These pieces were sent for examination to John Howard, who found no signs of an actual delivery when he visited her at home. Despite this, more animal parts—such as rabbit limbs, an eel's spine, and even cat legs—were delivered, drawing the attention of King George I's court.

King George sent Henry Davenant to investigate, and he became convinced of the bizarre events. Other members of the royal court were soon involved, witnessing Mary deliver more rabbit parts. One physician even believed the rabbits were bred by her. But when the King sent surgeon Cyriacus Ahlers to investigate, he was skeptical. Ahlers observed Mary attempting to prevent something from falling out by squeezing her legs together and noticed John Howard blocking his view during deliveries.

Ahlers made a crucial discovery—some animal parts had been cut with a knife. Mary was brought to London, where she continued her "deliveries" in front of medical experts. During one such event, she expelled a pig's bladder, but her swollen abdomen raised suspicions.

The story gained widespread attention in England, with many believing the hoax. It unraveled when it was revealed that Mary's husband, Joshua Toft, had been buying rabbits.

After days of questioning, Mary confessed that a friend had advised her to insert animal parts into her body for fame and fortune. Although she never gained money, Mary Toft became infamous, a notoriety that lasted until her death in 1763.

THE VERVE OF VOLTAIRE

The 18th-century French writer Voltaire lived a life filled with controversy and rebellion. Known for his sharp criticism of religion and authority, many of his works were banned in France for their anti-religious themes. His first major brush with controversy came in the late 1710s when he accused the Duc of Orleans of having an incestuous relationship with his own daughter. This led to Voltaire being imprisoned in the Bastille for nearly a year.

Though he was a fierce critic of others, Voltaire was no stranger to hypocrisy. He was also involved in an affair with his own niece. In 1729, he and a friend began buying lottery tickets in France, quickly realizing that the combined cost of the tickets was less than the total potential winnings. They purchased all the tickets and won every time, making Voltaire a millionaire.

Voltaire later became a Freemason, persuaded by his friend, Benjamin Franklin. As he approached death in 1778, Voltaire's final moments were as defiant as his life.

When a priest came to his bedside and urged him to renounce Satan, Voltaire's legendary response was, "Now, now, my good man. This is no time for making enemies." His wit and boldness lived on, even in his final moments.

THE BEAR WOMAN

Julia Pastrana was born in Mexico in 1834 with two rare conditions: hypertrichosis, which covered her face with thick black hair, and gingival hyperplasia, which gave her unusually large teeth, lips, and ears.

In 1854, she was sold to a circus and brought to the United States, where she was exhibited in freak shows under names like "The Bear Woman" and "The Ape Woman." Despite being exploited for her appearance, she captivated audiences around the world.

In 1857, Julia married Theodore Lent, a man who saw her more as a business opportunity than a wife. He was particularly interested in the possibility of passing on her rare features to their children. Standing just 4 feet 5 inches tall, Julia continued to perform, even as her personal life grew increasingly tragic.

While performing in Moscow, Julia gave birth to a son who inherited her distinctive features. Sadly, the child died after three days, and Julia herself passed away five days later due to complications from childbirth.

After her death, Theodore Lent sold the bodies of both Julia and her son to a Moscow doctor, who preserved them through taxidermy. Their remains were later studied by Charles Darwin and displayed in freak shows until 1972. It wasn't until 2013—150 years later—that Julia was finally laid to rest with a proper burial.

STALIN'S ISLAND GETAWAY

In 1933, Soviet dictator Joseph Stalin ordered 6,700 prisoners to be sent to Nazino Island in Siberia, with the goal of establishing a settlement. The majority of these prisoners were peasants whom Stalin viewed as undesirable. They were abandoned on the remote island with almost no food, supplies, or tools for survival. Within days, illness and despair spread, prompting some prisoners to attempt escape. However, the guards saw this as an opportunity for "human hunting," mercilessly pursuing and killing those who tried to flee.

As food supplies dwindled, desperation took hold. Prisoners formed gangs, preying on the weaker individuals to steal their meager rations. When the food ran out entirely, cannibalism became a horrifying reality, with the strongest turning on the weakest to survive. In one chilling incident, a woman managed to escape on a makeshift raft and reached a nearby house. When her rescuers found her, they were horrified to discover that her calves had been cut off and consumed by other prisoners.

Over the course of just three months, approximately 2,000 prisoners died from starvation, while another 2,000 mysteriously "disappeared," likely victims of cannibalism or brutal violence. Determined to conceal the atrocities, Stalin's regime actively suppressed information about the Nazino Island tragedy. It wasn't until 1988 that the true horrors of what occurred on the island were finally revealed to the world, exposing one of the darkest chapters of Soviet history.

LISZTOMANIA

F ranz Liszt was a legendary composer who took Europe by storm in the 1840s. Trained by his father, Adam—who was a close friend of Beethoven—Liszt began touring at an astonishingly young age. During his journeys, he befriended influential composers like Frédéric Chopin and Richard Wagner, the latter of whom would later become romantically involved with Liszt's teenage daughter.

Beyond his extraordinary musical talent, Liszt's striking looks and charismatic presence fueled a wave of fanaticism wherever he performed. Admirers were so enchanted that they collected keepsakes such as locks of his hair, discarded cigar butts, and even crafted jewelry from his belongings.

Aware of his magnetic appeal, Liszt revolutionized concert performance by choosing to play in profile, intentionally allowing his female fans a clear view of his face. This innovative stage presence set the standard for modern concert performances, influencing how artists engage with audiences to this day.

Long before Beatlemania swept the world, Liszt inspired "Lisztomania"—a term coined to describe the frenzied adoration and near-hysteria that followed him throughout his career.

Oddities

MUMMY, IT'S WHAT'S FOR DINNER

Trends and fads may come and go, but in Victorian England, the upper class was captivated by one of the most macabre spectacles in history: mummy unwrapping parties. At lavish social gatherings, it was not uncommon for a large, ornate box to be placed on display. To the amazement of the assembled guests, the box would be opened to reveal a genuine Egyptian mummy. The host, often a medical professional or antiquarian, would meticulously peel away the ancient linen wrappings, gradually exposing the 3,000-year-old remains beneath.

Europe's fascination with mummies, however, dated back centuries. In Shakespearean times, ground-up mummies were believed to have medicinal properties, and people even ingested them as remedies for ailments like headaches. Later, after Napoleon's campaigns in Egypt, French aristocrats popularized the practice of bringing mummies back as exotic souvenirs, further igniting Europe's obsession with these ancient relics.

These mummy unwrapping parties were more than just eerie entertainment; some attendees believed that consuming powdered mummy parts could provide health benefits. By the early 1900s, the trend began to decline, but not before thousands of mummies were plundered from their tombs, unwrapped at extravagant gatherings, or consumed for their supposed healing powers. This bizarre Victorian obsession reflects a time when science, superstition, and spectacle were bizarrely intertwined, leaving a curious and haunting mark on history.

BENGA IN THE BRONX

In the late 19th century, a Christian missionary named Samuel Phillips Warner traveled to the Congo region of Africa, where he encountered a young Congolese boy named Ota Benga. After discovering that Ota Benga's entire tribe had been massacred by the Belgian colonial forces, Warner decided to take him to the United States.

Ota Benga was paraded across the country as part of a traveling exhibit before being placed in the Bronx Zoo in New York City as a human curiosity. At the zoo, he was displayed in the Monkey House exhibit, where he was forced to lie in a hammock and perform by shooting arrows at targets set up around his enclosure.

Longing to return to his homeland, Ota Benga was once told that he would soon be able to go back to the Congo. However, his hopes were shattered when the outbreak of World War I prevented his return. Consumed by despair and isolation, Ota Benga built a ceremonial fire on March 20, 1916, and ended his life by shooting himself in the chest at the age of 32.

His tragic story stands as a haunting reminder of the inhumanity and exploitation faced by many during the colonial era.

Oddities

THE TALK SHOW AND THE TRAGEDY

On July 24, 1915, employees of the Western Electric Company in Cicero, Illinois, boarded the SS Eastland for a company picnic bound for Michigan City, Indiana. That morning, over 2,500 passengers crowded onto the ship, far exceeding its maximum capacity.

While still docked along the banks of the Chicago River, many passengers rushed to one side to wave goodbye to the crowd on shore. The sudden shift in weight caused the ship to tip violently before fully capsizing. In the ensuing chaos, 844 people lost their lives, making it one of the deadliest maritime disasters in American history.

Rescue teams arrived quickly, recovering bodies from the river and transporting them to a nearby warehouse. The building was used as a temporary morgue where families and loved ones came to identify the victims.

Nearly 70 years later, this same warehouse was converted into a television studio—Harpo Studios, owned by Oprah Winfrey.

Since the studio's opening, several employees working on Oprah's iconic television show have reported eerie encounters, including sightings of apparitions believed to be the spirits of those who perished in the SS Eastland disaster.

The tragic history of the SS Eastland continues to linger, casting a haunting presence over the site where so many lives were lost.

PARROT LEATHER

In 1878, in Wyoming, a man known as "Big Nose" George Parrott attempted to rob a train. During the failed heist, he murdered a sheriff and a detective before eventually being captured. When Parrott was jailed, a furious mob of over 200 people stormed the prison, dragged him from his cell, and lynched him from a telegraph pole in an act of vigilante justice.

Intrigued by the possibility of finding a neurological explanation for Parrott's criminal behavior, a Wyoming doctor named John Osborne decided to study his brain. During the examination, Dr. Osborne removed the top of Parrott's skull and gifted it to his 16-year-old assistant, Lillian Heath. Remarkably, Heath later became one of the first female doctors in the western United States—and she reportedly used the skull cap as an ashtray.

After finding no clues in Parrott's brain, Dr. Osborne went a step further by removing large portions of skin from the outlaw's body. He tanned the skin and crafted it into a pair of human leather shoes. Years later, Dr. Osborne wore these unsettling shoes to his inauguration ball when he was sworn in as the Governor of Wyoming in 1893.

PART 2

POP CULTURE

CHAPTER 1

THE NOT-SO GOLDEN AGE OF HOLLYWOOD

THE FIRST CHILD STAR

John Leslie Coogan was born in Los Angeles on October 26, 1914, and wasted no time stepping into the spotlight. By 1917, he had already made his film debut and was also performing in vaudeville, where his talent caught the eye of Charlie Chaplin. Recognizing the young performer's potential, Chaplin cast him in A Day's Pleasure, but it was The Kid that truly launched Jackie Coogan into superstardom. At just four years old, he delivered one of the most iconic child performances in cinematic history, becoming one of the first child actors to captivate audiences worldwide.

Coogan's rapid rise to fame led to a string of high-profile roles, including the title character in Oliver Twist, alongside legendary actor Lon Chaney. By the mid-1920s, he was more than just a movie star—his face was plastered on advertisements for peanut butter, toys, and school supplies, making him a household name. By the time he turned 21, Coogan had amassed an estimated $4 million—the equivalent of about $52 million today.

However, his fortune would soon vanish. After his father's tragic death in a car accident, Coogan discovered that his mother and her new husband, Arthur Bernstein, had squandered nearly all of his earnings. Bernstein, who had also been the family's financial advisor, had left him with virtually nothing.

In 1938, Coogan took legal action, suing his mother and stepfather. However, he was awarded only $126,000, a fraction of what he had earned.

The case sparked national outrage, leading to the passage of the Coogan Act in 1939, a law requiring that 15% of a child actor's earnings be placed in a trust to prevent similar exploitation.

Coogan's personal life was marked by more tragedy. In 1933, his college friend Brooke Hart was kidnapped and murdered. When the suspects were captured, a mob of enraged citizens—including Coogan—stormed the jail and lynched the kidnappers, an act of vigilante justice that made national headlines.

Despite struggling to reclaim his early stardom, Coogan eventually found a new place in pop culture history.

In 1964, he took on the beloved role of Uncle Fester in The Addams Family, reintroducing himself to a new generation of fans and securing his legacy in entertainment history.

THE FIRST MOVIE STAR

Florence Lawrence, born in 1886 in Hamilton, Ontario, is widely regarded as the first true movie star—though, ironically, she was initially unknown by name. In the early days of Hollywood, studios deliberately kept actors anonymous, fearing that individual recognition would lead to demands for higher salaries. However, Lawrence's immense popularity eventually forced the industry to acknowledge its stars, making her the first actress to receive on-screen credit.

Lawrence's career began in childhood, but her breakthrough came in 1906 when she entered the burgeoning film industry. She quickly became a favorite of director D.W. Griffith, starring in an astonishing 60 films within three years. Though audiences adored her, she was only known as the "Biograph Girl," as actors at the time remained unnamed.

In 1909, film producer Carl Laemmle recognized Lawrence's potential and brought her to his newly established Independent Moving Pictures Company (IMP).

To generate buzz, Laemmle orchestrated an outrageous publicity stunt, falsely reporting that Lawrence had died in a streetcar accident. Days later, she reappeared alive, creating a media sensation and securing her place as the first credited movie star.

Lawrence's fame skyrocketed, but tragedy soon followed. In 1915, she suffered severe injuries on set, including burns and a fractured spine.

Unable to work and abandoned by the studios, her once-thriving career collapsed. Though she made a brief return to acting, opportunities were scarce, and financial struggles mounted.

On December 28, 1938, at the age of 52, Lawrence was found dead from an apparent suicide. Despite her tragic end, she left behind a lasting legacy, paving the way for future generations of actresses and forever changing the way Hollywood treated its stars.

IN LIKE FLYNN

Errol Flynn, born in 1909 in Tasmania, Australia, was known for his adventurous roles in films, but his off-screen life was anything but heroic. A notorious heavy drinker and womanizer, Flynn's reckless behavior was legendary in Hollywood. In 1942, he was accused of statutory rape by two underage girls, but he was acquitted of all charges, thanks to his fame and status. This event led to the creation of the term "in like Flynn," a reference to his ability to evade consequences for his criminal actions.

Flynn's personal life was even more disturbing. His home was designed with voyeuristic features like two-way mirrors, peepholes, and hidden passages, allowing him to spy on guests without them knowing. His sexual preferences, particularly for underage girls, were an open secret, and he often involved others, including future Scientology founder L. Ron Hubbard, in his sordid escapades.

In the final years of his life, Flynn settled down with his 17-year-old girlfriend, Beverly Aadland. During this period, he became fascinated by the Cuban Revolution and traveled to Cuba to witness it firsthand.

He even befriended Fidel Castro and filmed the disaster that became Cuban Rebel Girls. The film, one of Flynn's worst, mirrored his chaotic life, and his time in Cuba ended with him witnessing executions before leaving due to his failing health.

Flynn died in 1959 at age 50 from a heart attack, but his story didn't end there. During his autopsy, doctors discovered genital warts, which were later removed and preserved in formaldehyde as a grotesque keepsake. Flynn's tragic legacy extended to his son, Sean, who was kidnapped and likely murdered while working as a war photographer in Cambodia during the Vietnam War.

THE LEGEND AND THE LOVE-CHILD

During the filming of Call of the Wild in 1935, Hollywood stars Clark Gable and Loretta Young engaged in a brief, secret affair—one that led to an unexpected pregnancy. The situation was especially complicated since Gable was married at the time, and for 22-year-old Young, an unwed pregnancy could have destroyed her career. Under immense pressure from the studio to protect her reputation, Young discreetly left for England, where she gave birth in secret and arranged for the baby to be placed for adoption.

Nearly two years later, Young made headlines when she adopted a 19-month-old girl named Judy—without publicly acknowledging that the child was, in fact, her own biological daughter. As Judy grew older, her striking resemblance to Clark Gable became increasingly difficult to ignore. When she was seven, Young, desperate to conceal the truth, had her undergo a painful procedure to pin back her ears in an attempt to lessen the likeness to Gable.

Their relationship remained complicated. Young, burdened by guilt and shame over the scandal, allegedly referred to Judy as a "walking mortal sin," a painful reminder of a past she tried to bury. Despite this, Judy lived with the weight of her mother's choices, growing up in the shadow of a secret that had been designed to protect Young's Hollywood legacy.

A BIBLICAL DISASTER

The 1928 epic Noah's Ark, directed by Michael Curtiz was promoted as "The Spectacle for the Ages!" A disaster film of unprecedented scale, it aimed to leave a lasting impact. Beyond its massive budget and status as one of the first talkies, Noah's Ark was particularly groundbreaking for its ambitious practical effects—most notably, its infamous flood scene.

Director Michael Curtiz was determined to make the flood sequence as realistic as possible. Teaming up with producer and writer Darryl Zanuck, Curtiz devised a daring and reckless plan: they would unleash 600,000 gallons of water onto a set packed with 7,500 extras to achieve an authentic sense of chaos and destruction. However, in a move that would prove disastrous, Curtiz deliberately withheld crucial details from the extras, refusing to tell them when or from which direction the deluge would hit.

Cinematographer Hal Mohr voiced his alarm, confronting Curtiz with the question, "Jesus, what are you going to do about the extras?" Curtiz's chilling response: "They're going to have to take their chances." Furious, Mohr stormed off the set and refused to return.

The set itself was a massive concrete basin filled with extras and live animals. When the flood was finally released, a powerful torrent of freezing water came crashing down without warning, sweeping through the set with devastating force. Panic ensued as people were tossed and battered by the violent current.

Many suffered serious injuries—several extras broke bones, one had a leg so badly mangled it required amputation, and tragically, three people drowned. It took 35 ambulances to transport the injured.

Among the extras caught in the chaos was a young aspiring actor named Marion Morrison—who would later become known as John Wayne.

Despite the horrific conditions and loss of life, no legal action was taken against Curtiz or Warner Bros. The studio downplayed the incident, dismissing reports of fatalities as exaggerated. Curtiz, undeterred by the disaster, continued his career unscathed, ultimately directing Casablanca, one of the most celebrated films of all time. However, the Noah's Ark flood remains one of Hollywood's most tragic and reckless on-set disasters—an era-defining example of the industry's disregard for safety in pursuit of spectacle.

WHALE IN THE WATER

In 1931, Frankenstein director James Whale entered into a long-term relationship with producer David Lewis. The two shared a home and remained partners for 16 years. However, in 1947, while traveling in France, the 62-year-old Whale met a 25-year-old bartender named Pierre Foegel at a gay bar. Instantly infatuated, he began a romantic relationship with Pierre.

Upon returning to the United States, Whale informed Lewis of his intention to bring Pierre over from France and pursue a polyamorous relationship. Lewis firmly rejected the idea, leading to the end of their long-standing partnership. After Lewis's departure, Whale became known for hosting lavish, all-male pool parties at his home, adding to his reputation for extravagant social gatherings.

Ironically, despite his love for poolside entertaining, Whale had a deep fear of water and never learned to swim. Still, he had a swimming pool built in his backyard. As the years passed, his health began to decline following a debilitating stroke.

During his recovery, he developed a romantic attachment to his male live-in nurse. Pierre, jealous of this new bond, demanded that the nurse be replaced with a woman.

Struggling with failing health, emotional turmoil, and the dissolution of his relationships, Whale made a tragic decision. On May 29, 1957, at the age of 67, he walked to his backyard pool and ended his life by drowning. His death marked a sorrowful end to an extraordinary life—one filled with artistic brilliance, complicated relationships, and deep personal struggles.

THE LIFE OF DOROTHY GIBSON

Dorothy Brown, born on May 17, 1889, in Hoboken, New Jersey, first found success as a vaudeville singer and dancer before transitioning into modeling. Her striking beauty and stage presence soon led her to acting, where she quickly rose to prominence. By 1911, she was landing small film roles, and within a year, she became one of the earliest actresses to be recognized as a true movie star.

In 1912, while vacationing in Italy with her mother, Dorothy's husband, film industry mogul Jules Brulatour, urged her to return home earlier than planned. She booked passage on the RMS Titanic, unaware that the voyage would become one of the most infamous in history. While playing cards with friends on board, the ship struck an iceberg. Dorothy managed to secure a spot on one of the first lifeboats to be launched, but it had a leak. In a desperate effort to stay afloat, she and the other women stuffed the hole with their lingerie until they were rescued by the Carpathia.

Despite the trauma, Dorothy returned to New York and, remarkably, starred in Saved From the Titanic just a month later.

She not only played the lead role but also wrote the screenplay and wore the very clothes she had on during the disaster. However, at the height of her career, she made the shocking decision to retire from acting that same year.

Seeking a quieter life, Dorothy relocated to Paris before eventually settling in Florence, Italy. Her story took an unexpected turn when she became a supporter of Benito Mussolini's fascist regime and later worked as a Nazi spy during World War II.

In 1944, disillusioned with fascism, she attempted to break ties but was arrested by Mussolini's government. She managed to escape prison and fled back to Paris, where she died from a heart attack at the age of 56—leaving behind a life as dramatic and unpredictable as the films she once starred in.

SEARCHING FOR BOBBY DRISCOLL

Long before Shia LaBeouf, Miley Cyrus, or even Kurt Russell found fame as Disney child stars, Bobby Driscoll was one of the studio's earliest and brightest talents. He rose to prominence in the late 1940s and early 1950s, earning acclaim for his performances in films like Song of the South and Treasure Island. However, he was best known as the voice of Peter Pan in Disney's 1953 animated classic. During his early years, Walt Disney personally took an interest in his career, providing him with opportunities that many young actors could only dream of. Unfortunately, as Driscoll grew older, severe acne drastically changed his appearance, making it difficult for him to maintain his childlike image. As a result, Disney abruptly ended its association with him, effectively ending his Hollywood career.

Struggling to find work, Driscoll turned to drugs, eventually becoming addicted to heroin. He moved to New York City, where he became involved with the underground art scene and associated with figures such as Andy Warhol. However, his addiction overshadowed his once-promising career, leaving him penniless and estranged from his family.

In 1969, Driscoll's mother, desperate for answers, contacted Disney in an effort to locate her missing son. Tragically, she learned that he had died over a year earlier. On March 30, 1968, two young boys exploring an abandoned tenement in New York City stumbled upon a lifeless body on a worn-out mattress.

Authorities determined that the man had died from heart failure caused by prolonged drug use, but with no identification on him, he was buried in an unmarked pauper's grave.

It wasn't until later that his fingerprints were matched to his records, allowing his mother to finally discover his fate—far from the bright spotlight in which he had once thrived.

THE INCREDIBLE LIFE OF JOHN CHAMBERS

Many soldiers returned from World War II with devastating injuries, including missing limbs and severe facial trauma. To help them regain a sense of normalcy, advancements in prosthetics became crucial. One of the key figures in revolutionizing prosthetic design for veterans was John Chambers, born on September 12, 1922, in Chicago, Illinois.

Chambers served as a dental technician in the U.S. Army, where he witnessed the horrific effects of war firsthand. After returning home, he dedicated himself to developing prosthetic limbs and facial reconstruction devices for wounded veterans, helping them rebuild their lives.

During this time, Chambers crossed paths with Hollywood makeup artist Ben Nye, an encounter that introduced him to the world of film and television. In 1953, he was hired by NBC as a makeup artist, a role that eventually led him to Universal Pictures, where he became known for his work on The Munsters, a popular television show.

In 1966, 20th Century Fox began developing a film adaptation of Twilight Zone creator Rod Serling's Planet of the Apes. After numerous script and casting changes, the studio needed a makeup artist capable of creating hyper-realistic ape characters. Chambers was chosen for the job, having already gained recognition for his work on Star Trek, where he designed Leonard Nimoy's iconic Spock ears.

His groundbreaking prosthetic makeup techniques played a major role in the success of Planet of the Apes, earning him an honorary Oscar in 1969.

Chambers' career took an unexpected turn when he was recruited by CIA agent Tony Mendez in 1979 during the Iranian Hostage Crisis. Mendez enlisted Chambers to help create fake identities and disguises for CIA agents in a covert mission to rescue six American hostages. The operation, later known as Argo, was a success, and Chambers was quietly honored by the CIA for his role in the mission.

John Chambers passed away in 2001, but his remarkable legacy endures. His contributions to film, prosthetics, and espionage were immortalized when John Goodman portrayed him in the 2012 film Argo, which went on to win the Academy Award for Best Picture.

From transforming war veterans' lives to reshaping Hollywood special effects—and even aiding in international espionage—John Chambers' story is one of extraordinary talent, ingenuity, and impact.

CHAPTER 2

POP CULTURE CRIME SPREE

BRUCE LEE: THE MASS MURDERER?

On the night of August 8, 1969, actress Sharon Tate hosted a gathering at her Los Angeles home with friends Jay Sebring, Wojciech Frykowski, and Abigail Folger. At 8½ months pregnant, Tate was eagerly awaiting the birth of her first child with director Roman Polanski, who was away in Europe working on a film. That evening, actor Steve McQueen and music producer Quincy Jones had been invited but ultimately chose not to attend—a fortunate decision given the horrors that would soon unfold.

That night, followers of cult leader Charles Manson—Tex Watson, Susan Atkins, Patricia Krenwinkel, and Linda Kasabian—arrived at the property with orders to kill everyone inside. The brutal murders shocked the nation and became one of the most infamous crimes in U.S. history.

In the aftermath, the police had little evidence to work with, leaving the case unsolved for months. A devastated Polanski took it upon himself to investigate, secretly monitoring his friends and even swabbing car doors for blood to find a match.

One clue that caught his attention was a pair of glasses found at the crime scene, which didn't belong to any of the victims. While training at Paramount Studios, Polanski's martial arts instructor, Bruce Lee, casually mentioned misplacing a pair of glasses, leading Polanski to briefly suspect him. To confirm, Polanski offered to take Lee to an ophthalmologist, but the prescription did not match, ruling him out.

Eventually, Manson and his followers were arrested, convicted, and sentenced to death—a punishment later commuted to life in prison when California abolished the death penalty. In 1973, Bruce Lee died under mysterious circumstances, fueling speculation and conspiracy theories. Meanwhile, in 1977, Polanski was indicted for the sexual assault of a minor. To avoid sentencing, he fled the United States and has remained in exile ever since.

TERMINATOR 2: BEHIND THE SCENES

James Cameron's *The Terminator*, inspired by a nightmare he had of a relentless killing machine, debuted in 1984 and quickly became a cult classic, grossing $78.4 million. The film launched the careers of both Cameron and its star, Arnold Schwarzenegger. Its success paved the way for Cameron to direct *Aliens* and *The Abyss*, solidifying his reputation as a visionary filmmaker and fueling demand for a *Terminator* sequel.

For *Terminator 2: Judgment Day*, Cameron reimagined Schwarzenegger's character as the hero, necessitating a new villain—the shape-shifting, liquid-metal T-1000. Originally, rock legend Billy Idol was considered for the role, but a motorcycle accident forced him to drop out before filming. Ultimately, Robert Patrick was cast, bringing a chilling, steely presence to the character.

Filming for *T2* began in October 1990 and quickly became infamous for its grueling production. Cameron's relentless pursuit of perfection meant endless takes and exhausting hours, pushing the cast and crew to their limits. One of the film's most memorable moments—the biker bar scene, where a naked Schwarzenegger demands clothes—was shot at the Corral Bar in Los Angeles on March 3, 1991.

Unbeknownst to those on set, a historic event was unfolding just nearby that same night. George Holliday, a local resident who had been filming behind-the-scenes footage of the movie on his home video camera, inadvertently captured a different scene—LAPD officers brutally beating Rodney King after a high-speed chase.

When Holliday released the footage to the media, it ignited national outrage. The subsequent acquittal of the officers in 1992 triggered the infamous LA riots, marking a pivotal moment in American history.

CATHARINE'S CLOSE CALL

In November 1977, a 24-year-old woman named Catharine Lorre was approached by two men in police uniforms while walking in Los Angeles. They struck up a brief conversation before asking to see her driver's license. Without hesitation, she handed it over, and after a quick glance, the officers returned it and let her go. To Catharine, the encounter seemed routine—nothing out of the ordinary.

Two years later, however, she was watching the news when a chilling realization hit her. The faces of two recently arrested serial killers looked eerily familiar. To her horror, they were the same "officers" who had stopped her that night. The men, Angelo Buono and Kenneth Bianchi, had been posing as police while committing a string of brutal murders in Los Angeles, eventually becoming infamous as the *Hillside Stranglers*. Unbeknownst to Catharine at the time, Buono and Bianchi had intended to abduct and kill her that night.

However, as they examined her driver's license, they noticed a childhood photo of her with her father—Peter Lorre, the legendary actor best known for playing a serial killer in the 1931 film *M*. Both men were fans of Lorre's films, particularly his chilling portrayals of murderers, and feared that harming the child of a Hollywood star would attract too much attention. Deciding it was too risky, they let her go.

Kenneth Bianchi is currently serving a life sentence in Washington State Penitentiary for the Hillside Strangler murders, as well as two additional killings in Washington.

His accomplice, Angelo Buono, died of a heart attack in 2002 while serving his sentence. Tragically, Catharine Lorre passed away in 1985 from complications of diabetes at the age of 32, forever unaware of just how close she had come to becoming another victim of the Hillside Stranglers.

ROTTEN'S REPLACEMENT

The Sex Pistols became notorious in the UK for their chaotic performances and rebellious antics, including swearing on live television. After releasing their only studio album, *Never Mind the Bollocks, Here's the Sex Pistols*, in 1977, they embarked on a disastrous U.S. tour that led to the band's implosion. Frontman Johnny Rotten and bassist Sid Vicious both quit, leaving drummer Paul Cook and guitarist Steve Jones to pick up the pieces. In search of a new frontman, they turned to an unlikely candidate—Ronnie Biggs, who was living in Brazil to evade extradition.

Biggs was no rock star—he was a fugitive. A key figure in the infamous 1963 Great Train Robbery, he and 14 accomplices stole what would be equivalent to $70 million today. His downfall came when police linked his fingerprints to a *Monopoly* board left at the crime scene, leading to his arrest. However, Biggs escaped prison in 1965 and fled to Brazil, where he took advantage of the country's refusal to extradite British criminals.

Despite his criminal past, Biggs collaborated with the remaining Sex Pistols, recording the song "No One Is Innocent," an anarchic anthem that blended punk rebellion with outlaw infamy—further cementing the band's legacy of controversy.

RICKLES' CLOSE CALL

Don Rickles was born on May 8, 1926, in Queens, New York. After serving in World War II, he set his sights on acting and stand-up comedy, honing his craft in New York City's bustling nightclub scene. It was during these early performances that he encountered Frank Sinatra, sparking a friendship that lasted until Sinatra's passing in 1998. Rickles' sharp wit and fearless humor propelled him to success, leading to his 1958 film debut in *Run Silent, Run Deep* and his memorable role in *Kelly's Heroes* (1970). He also became a television staple, making legendary appearances on *The Tonight Show* and the *Dean Martin Roasts*, where he perfected his signature insult comedy.

In 1972, Rickles had a brush with danger that could have changed his life forever. On the night of April 3, he was set to perform at the famous Copacabana nightclub in New York. Moments before stepping on stage, he was warned that notorious mobster Joe Gallo was in the audience and advised to steer clear of him. Known as *Crazy Joe*, Gallo had a long history of violent crime, had recently been released from prison, and was deeply entangled in ongoing mob wars.

Despite the warning, Rickles refused to alter his act and launched into his usual brand of cutting humor—targeting Gallo in front of the entire crowd. Instead of taking offense, the feared gangster laughed and enjoyed the performance. Impressed, he even invited Rickles to join him for dinner at Umberto's Clam House in Little Italy. Rickles declined, unaware that later that night, Gallo would be gunned down by mafia hitmen in a barrage of bullets.

Dodging those literal bullets, Rickles continued his long and successful career, cementing his legacy as one of comedy's greatest pioneers. He remained active in show business until his passing in 2017 at the age of 90, having spent a lifetime proving that no one—not even the mob—was safe from his razor-sharp wit.

HOLLYWOOD AND THE MOB: A LOVE STORY

Harry Cohn, born on July 23, 1891, in New York City, climbed the ranks of the film industry through a combination of ambition, cunning, and sheer ruthlessness. After working a series of odd jobs, he secured a position with Independent Moving Pictures through his brother, Jack Cohn. This led to a role as a personal secretary to Carl Laemmle, president of Universal Pictures, providing Cohn with an inside look at the power dynamics of Hollywood. Eventually, he became one of the driving forces behind the formation of Columbia Pictures, a studio he ruled with an iron fist.

Cohn's reputation as a tyrant was infamous. His office famously displayed an autographed photo of Benito Mussolini, a reflection of his dictatorial management style. He was also a key figure in the Hollywood "casting couch" culture, often demanding sexual favors from actresses in exchange for coveted film roles. His aggressive pursuit of control extended beyond the film industry—he secured financial backing from mob boss Abner Zwillman, strengthening his grip on Columbia and solidifying his deep ties to organized crime.

These connections would later inspire the character Jack Woltz in *The Godfather*. One of Cohn's most notorious scandals erupted in 1957 when he sought to suppress the interracial romance between actor Sammy Davis Jr. and Columbia starlet Kim Novak. Fearing backlash and damage to Novak's career, Cohn turned to the mafia for assistance, enlisting John Roselli, a mobster with strong ties to both Hollywood and organized crime, to "handle" the situation.

Roselli's influence extended far beyond Hollywood. He became involved in CIA-backed plots to assassinate Fidel Castro, acting as a liaison between the intelligence community and the mafia. His underworld connections would later intertwine with the Kennedy assassination conspiracy. In 1976, as Roselli was set to testify about these covert operations, he disappeared. Weeks later, his dismembered body was found stuffed in a steel drum floating off the coast of Miami—one of the most infamous mob hits in history.

Cohn, however, did not meet such a violent end. He died of a heart attack in 1958, leaving behind a legacy of corruption, intimidation, and power plays that shaped the darker side of Hollywood's Golden Age.

ENOUGH IS ENOUGH

Lana Turner, one of Hollywood's most glamorous stars of the 1950s, saw her personal life become entangled in scandal and tragedy. In 1957, she began a volatile relationship with Johnny Stompanato, a bodyguard for Los Angeles mob boss Mickey Cohen and a notorious enforcer. From the outset, their romance was marred by Stompanato's violent temper and jealousy, creating a storm of conflict behind the scenes.

While Turner was filming *Another Time, Another Place* in London, Stompanato's possessiveness took a dangerous turn. Suspecting an affair between Turner and her co-star Sean Connery, he flew to the set and confronted the rising actor. Brandishing a gun, he threatened Connery—only to be swiftly disarmed and knocked unconscious by the future James Bond, cementing Connery's real-life tough-guy reputation.

The following year would mark both a career high and a personal nightmare for Turner. Fresh off an Oscar nomination for Best Actress, her relationship with Stompanato spiraled into violence. On the night of April 4, 1958, a heated argument erupted in Turner's Beverly Hills home.

Fearing for her mother's safety, Turner's 14-year-old daughter, Cheryl Crane, grabbed a kitchen knife and stabbed Stompanato in the stomach, killing him.

The ensuing investigation ruled Stompanato's death a justifiable homicide, citing self-defense. Cheryl was released without legal consequences, but the case became one of Hollywood's most infamous scandals. Despite the personal turmoil, Turner's resilience and unforgettable performances solidified her legacy as one of cinema's most enduring icons.

YEP, YEP, YEP

Judith Barsi was born in Los Angeles in 1978 to Hungarian immigrants Joseph and Maria Barsi. From an early age, she showed remarkable talent, launching her acting career at just five years old. She quickly became a rising star, appearing in over 70 commercials and landing roles in popular television shows like *Punky Brewster*. With her charm and natural ability, she seemed destined for a bright future in Hollywood.

However, behind the scenes, Judith's home life was a nightmare. Her father, Joseph, was an abusive alcoholic who terrorized the family with violence and threats. He frequently warned that he would kill his wife, his daughter, and himself, creating an environment of constant fear.

Tragically, his threats became reality on July 25, 1988. In a horrific act of violence, Joseph fatally shot his wife, Maria, and their 10-year-old daughter before taking his own life. The murder-suicide shattered the life of a promising young actress whose career had only just begun.

Months after her death, Judith's voice echoed on the big screen in *The Land Before Time*, the animated classic produced by Steven Spielberg. She had brought to life the lovable character Ducky, whose joyful catchphrase—*"YEP! YEP! YEP!"*—became iconic. Today, those words are engraved on Judith's grave marker, a bittersweet tribute to the talent and happiness she shared with the world despite the darkness she endured.

WHAT MOMMA DON'T KNOW...

Russ Columbo was a singer and actor who rose to national fame in the 1930s, helping to popularize the crooning style alongside contemporaries like Bing Crosby. His smooth vocals and Hollywood charm made him a rising star, but his life was cut tragically short in a freak accident.

On September 2, 1934, just before he was scheduled to have dinner with actress Carole Lombard, Columbo stopped by the home of his friend, Lancing Brown. While the two were examining Brown's firearm collection, disaster struck. A gun in Brown's hands accidentally discharged, firing a bullet that struck Columbo above his left eye, killing him instantly. His sudden death sent shockwaves through Hollywood and devastated those who knew him.

At the time, Columbo's mother was recovering from a major heart attack in the hospital. Fearing the news of his death would be too much for her to bear—and could possibly be fatal—his siblings made an agonizing decision: they chose not to tell her. Believing she only had a short time left, they crafted an elaborate deception to shield her from the truth.

However, Columbo's mother defied expectations and lived for another ten years. For an entire decade, his family kept up the illusion that he was still alive. They wrote letters in his name, played recordings of his voice, and assured her that he was busy with his successful radio career. In one of Hollywood's most surreal real-life stories, a mother was spared the heartbreak of losing her son by any means necessary.

CHAPTER 3

INCREDIBLE ORIGIN STORIES

THE BAND THAT COULD HAVE BEEN

Chevy Chase, born Cornelius Crane Chase, displayed a natural talent for comedy from an early age. His sharp wit and impeccable timing set him apart, paving the way for his rise as one of the most recognizable comedians of his generation. However, comedy wasn't his only gift—Chase was also a skilled musician, boasting perfect pitch and impressive drumming abilities. This lesser-known musical talent would later become part of one of pop culture's most fascinating "what if" stories.

While attending Bard College in upstate New York, Chase often played music with fellow students, occasionally performing live gigs. One of the bands he briefly drummed for was a self-described "bad jazz band" called Leather Canary. However, his time with the group was cut short when he was expelled from Bard after an infamous prank involving a live cow in his dorm room.

After leaving college, Chase shifted his focus entirely to comedy, joining *The National Lampoon Radio Hour* before making history as part of the original cast of *Saturday Night Live* in 1975. His career skyrocketed after just one season, leading to iconic roles in *Caddyshack*, *Fletch*, and *National Lampoon's Vacation*.

Meanwhile, Leather Canary's remaining members—Donald Fagen and Walter Becker—decided to take their music in a new direction. Seeking a fresh identity, they drew inspiration from William S. Burroughs' novel *Naked Lunch*, naming their band Steely Dan after a steam-powered mechanical sex toy mentioned in the book. They would go on to become one of the most legendary rock bands of the 1970s, while Chase cemented his place in comedy history.

COMPLIMENTS TO THE CHEF

During World War II, the Office of Strategic Services (OSS) launched a research initiative known as the Emergency Sea Rescue Equipment Section, aimed at protecting American pilots who had been shot down over the ocean. One of their primary concerns was the threat of shark attacks, leading to the development of a specialized shark repellent.

Among the researchers was a young assistant who helped create a repellent "cake" made from copper acetate and black dye. The mixture was designed to release a scent mimicking that of a dead shark, a natural deterrent to live sharks. To the team's surprise, the formula proved effective, offering downed pilots an added layer of protection against marine predators.

That young assistant, whose early work in shark repellents remained largely unknown, would later become a beloved household name—Julia Child. Decades before revolutionizing American cooking with her television shows and cookbooks, Child played a small but fascinating role in wartime intelligence, adding yet another remarkable chapter to her extraordinary life.

AN UNLIKELY LOVE STORY

The story of Morris Weinrib and Mary Rubinstein is one of resilience, love, and survival in the face of unimaginable horror. When Nazi forces invaded Poland in 1939, Morris, a young Jewish man, was forced into the Starachowice ghetto. It was there that he met Mary, and amidst the darkness of war, their friendship grew into something deeper.

Their love was tested almost immediately when they were deported to Auschwitz, one of the most brutal extermination camps of the Holocaust. Even in such dire conditions, Morris found ways to express his devotion to Mary, bribing Nazi guards to secure small but significant comforts, such as a pair of shoes. Their bond became a source of strength, offering hope in a place designed to strip them of everything.

Their time together was cut short when Mary was transferred to Bergen-Belsen and Morris was sent to Dachau. The odds of either surviving were slim, and both feared they would never see each other again.

In 1945, as Allied forces liberated the camps, Morris emerged from Dachau and immediately set out to find Mary, clinging to the hope that she was still alive. Against all odds, he discovered that she had survived and was in a displaced persons camp. Reunited, the couple married and eventually immigrated to Canada, where they built a new life and raised a family.

In 1953, Mary gave birth to her and Morris's son, whom they named Gary Lee Weinrib. Due to her strong Polish accent, "Gary" often sounded like "Geddy," which led to Gary adopting the stage name Geddy Lee when he co-founded the seminal prog rock band Rush. Though Morris passed away when Geddy was still young, Mary lived long enough to see her son achieve international success. She passed away in 2021 at the age of 95, leaving behind not only her family's legacy but also a testament to the enduring power of love and survival.

MLK AND THE HOLLYWOOD ICON

During the 1960s, Georgia was a center of civil unrest and racial tensions, with segregation still deeply ingrained in the South. Many white Southerners fiercely resisted integration, keeping public institutions and schools divided. Amid this turbulent backdrop, a young couple from Smyrna, Georgia—Betty and Walter Roberts—challenged societal norms. As theater actors, they established the Atlanta Actors and Writers Workshop and a children's acting school in Decatur. Unlike most institutions at the time, their schools were fully integrated, welcoming children of all races in an era when such inclusivity was rare.

One of their students was Yolanda King, the daughter of civil rights leaders Dr. Martin Luther King Jr. and Coretta Scott King. Through their connection with the King family, the Roberts formed a close and lasting friendship with the prominent civil rights leaders. Despite facing their own financial struggles, Betty and Walter remained devoted to providing quality education and a nurturing community for all children.

In 1967, while expecting their third child, the Roberts faced mounting medical bills. However, they soon discovered that their hospital expenses had been quietly paid in full—by none other than Coretta and Dr. Martin Luther King Jr. Tragically, less than six months later, Dr. King was assassinated in Memphis.

That third child, born on October 28, 1967, was a daughter named Julia Roberts—who would grow up to become an Academy Award-winning actress. The generosity of the King family left a lasting imprint on the Roberts, shaping Julia's early life within a household that valued kindness, inclusion, and unity.

WHAT THE FUNK?

In 1963, legendary soul singer Otis Redding was performing at Club 15 in Macon, Georgia, captivating the audience with his electrifying presence. Among the crowd that night was Joe Tex, another prominent singer of the era. However, the lively atmosphere took a violent turn when a 29-year-old man stormed into the venue wielding two shotguns. Without hesitation, he opened fire on Joe Tex, sending the small club into chaos.

As panic spread, several people were injured—some from gunfire, others from stabbings amid the frantic commotion. The shooter later claimed his actions were fueled by jealousy and rivalry, believing Joe Tex to be a direct competitor. To suppress any fallout, the assailant's manager reportedly paid off witnesses, ensuring the incident remained hidden from the public eye.

The identity of the gunman? None other than James Brown, the man who would later be revered as the "Godfather of Soul."

Despite this violent episode in his early years, Brown went on to become one of the most influential figures in music history, leaving an indelible mark on generations of artists. Yet, this dark and seldom-discussed chapter remains one of the most startling moments in his rise to fame.

AS TENACIOUS AS IT GETS

On July 20, 1969, millions of Americans watched in awe as astronauts Neil Armstrong and Buzz Aldrin became the first humans to set foot on the moon, marking a historic victory in the Space Race. However, the next major lunar mission, Apollo 13, would face a life-threatening crisis.

Launched on April 11, 1970, astronauts James Lovell, Jack Swigert, and Fred Haise were forced to abort their mission after an oxygen tank ruptured, leaving them stranded in space. To survive, the crew relied on the Lunar Module's Abort Guidance System, which played a crucial role in their safe return to Earth on April 17, 1970.

One of the key engineers behind this life-saving system was Judith Love Cohen, born on August 16, 1933, in Brooklyn, New York. Exceptionally gifted in both math and engineering, she studied at Brooklyn College while also excelling as a ballet dancer. Despite the barriers for women in engineering at the time, she secured a position as a junior engineer at North American Aviation while attending the University of Southern California. She later earned a Master's degree in engineering in 1962.

Judith worked for Space Technology Laboratories, a NASA contractor, helping develop the Abort Guidance System for the Apollo Lunar Module. In 1969, during the Apollo 11 mission, she was eight months pregnant and actively solving a critical engineering problem. Even after going into labor, she brought her work with her to the hospital, completed the solution, and then called her boss to report both her success—and the birth of her baby boy.

That child would grow up to be actor and musician Jack Black. Judith Love Cohen's contributions to space exploration helped save lives, proving that brilliance and perseverance know no boundaries.

WHEELIN, DEALIN' N' BABY STEALIN'

In the mid-1920s, Georgia Tann was a social worker at the Tennessee Children's Home Society in Memphis, tasked with handling adoptions and placing children with new families. However, she soon realized there was a lucrative market in adoption and began exploiting the system, arranging out-of-state adoptions for wealthy couples willing to pay thousands of dollars for a child.

As demand grew, Tann ran out of children to sell. To keep her operation going, she began targeting poor, single mothers across Tennessee. She manipulated them into believing their children would have better lives elsewhere, never revealing her true intentions. Many unsuspecting mothers were deceived, unaware that Tann was trafficking their children for profit.

When persuasion no longer sufficed, Tann resorted to outright kidnapping. She stole infants from hospitals as well as from their own homes, falsifying records to cover her tracks. Her illegal adoption ring operated unchecked for 25 years, tearing thousands of families apart.

Tann's horrifying scheme was finally exposed in 1950, but she died of cancer that same year before facing justice. By the time of her death, she had kidnapped and sold over 5,000 children across the country, leaving behind a tragic legacy of stolen identities and shattered families.

Among those taken was an infant adopted by a young couple in Detroit, Kathleen and Richard Fleier. That child would grow up to become one of the most legendary professional wrestlers in history—Ric Flair. The dark legacy of Georgia Tann remains one of the most disturbing chapters in American adoption history, affecting countless lives, including that of one of wrestling's greatest icons.

FROM REVOLUTION TO DEVOLUTION

In the late 1960s and early 1970s, college campuses across the United States became hotbeds of anti-war protests as students voiced their opposition to America's escalating involvement in the Vietnam War. Tensions between demonstrators and authorities reached a tragic peak at Kent State University in Ohio. On May 4, 1970, the National Guard, deployed to disperse protesters, opened fire on the crowd, killing four students. Among the victims were Allison Krause and Jeffrey Miller, both close friends of Kent State student Gerald Casale.

The shocking event deeply affected Casale, leaving him disillusioned with the state of American society. Channeling his frustration into music, he partnered with his classmate Bob Lewis, and the two—both talented musicians—decided to form a band. They later recruited Mark Mothersbaugh, who was then playing in a separate band alongside another Kent State student, future Pretenders frontwoman Chrissie Hynde.

When searching for a name, Casale and Lewis reflected on the Kent State massacre as a symbol of societal decline.

They described the tragic events at Kent State University as a regression of humanity, or a *devolution* of society. Shortening the word, they named their band *DEVO*—a name that would become synonymous with their avant-garde music, satirical social commentary, and groundbreaking influence on new wave culture.

ROCK N ROLL SAVES LIVES

In the late 1950s and early 1960s, EMI was actively developing some of the first transistor computers and various electronic devices. However, by 1962, the company faced financial difficulties and was forced to shut down its computer division, led by Godfrey Hounsfield. Executives informed Hounsfield that his continued employment depended on an unexpected influx of funds.

At the same time, EMI was expanding into the music industry, recording albums for emerging British bands. Among them was a little-known group from Liverpool—The Beatles. When the band signed with EMI, their immense success generated a substantial revenue stream for the company.

This financial boost enabled Hounsfield to pursue his next project: developing the CT scanner, now known as the CAT scan. His groundbreaking invention later earned him the Nobel Prize for Medicine and has saved millions of lives—all made possible, in part, by The Beatles.

TEXAS ZOMBIES

One of the most pivotal moments in rock and roll history unfolded when a wave of British bands crossed the Atlantic, reshaping American youth culture forever. The Beatles, The Rolling Stones, The Who, and The Animals took inspiration from American blues musicians, infused it with their own British sensibilities, and left an indelible mark on the music industry. Their influence sparked a new generation of American bands eager to emulate their sound and forge their own legacies. While groups like The Beatles and The Rolling Stones achieved immense global fame, not all British Invasion acts reached the same heights. One such overlooked band was The Zombies.

Despite modest success in the UK, The Zombies struck gold in the United States with their 1969 hit "Time of the Season." The song dominated radio airwaves, seemingly priming the band for a triumphant U.S. tour. However, there was one major problem—the band had already broken up by the time the song gained popularity.

Sensing an opportunity, Delta Promotions, a Michigan-based company, devised a bold scheme. Knowing that most American fans wouldn't recognize The Zombies' actual members, they created not one, but two fake versions of the band—one in Michigan and another in Texas. The Texas version was particularly notable for being a four-piece instead of the original five-member lineup. When asked about the missing keyboardist, the impostors were instructed to claim he had been "busted and is now in jail." Surprisingly, the deception worked—at least for a while.

The charade unraveled when real Zombies bassist Chris White exposed the scam in a 1969 Rolling Stone interview, bringing the phony tours to an abrupt halt. Undeterred, Delta Promotions shifted its focus to manufacturing knockoff versions of other bands, including The Archies and The Animals.

But what became of the Texas Zombies? Two of its members, drummer Frank Beard and bassist Dusty Hill, went on to form the legendary rock band ZZ Top alongside guitarist Billy Gibbons. In an ironic twist, Beard remained clean-shaven while Hill and Gibbons grew their now-iconic beards. Their evolution from fake Zombies to bona fide rock legends is a testament to the strange and often absurd world of the music industry.

CHAPTER 4

STRANGE DEATHS

RUSSIAN ROULETTE GONE WRONG

Terry Kath, the exceptionally talented guitarist from Chicago, co-founded the band *Chicago Transit Authority* alongside fellow local musicians. In 1969, due to legal pressure from the actual Chicago Transit Authority, the band shortened its name to simply *Chicago*. Kath's innovative and soulful guitar work made him one of rock's most underrated musicians, but his struggles with drugs, alcohol, and a fascination with firearms created a dangerous mix.

On January 23, 1978, Kath's reckless habits led to a tragic accident. While hanging out with a band roadie, he began toying with a .38 revolver, playing a mock game of Russian Roulette to unsettle his companion. He repeatedly pulled the trigger of the empty gun, laughing off concerns. But Kath wasn't done—he picked up a 9mm pistol next, holding it to his head as he reassured the roadie, "Don't worry, the clip isn't in the gun."

While he was technically correct about the missing magazine, he overlooked one fatal detail: a single round remained in the chamber. His final words—"What do you think I'm gonna do, blow my brains out?"—proved tragically ironic. When he pulled the trigger, the gun fired, killing him instantly.

Terry Kath's life ended at just 31 years old, cutting short the career of a gifted musician whose groundbreaking guitar work left an indelible mark on rock history. His loss remains one of music's most heartbreaking tragedies.

THE TRAGIC END OF A SILVER SCREEN PSYCHO

Anthony Perkins is best remembered for his chilling portrayal of Norman Bates in Alfred Hitchcock's *Psycho* (1960), delivering one of the most iconic performances in film history. His career thrived throughout the 1960s and 1970s, and in 1973, he married photographer and actress Berinthia "Berry" Berenson. Together, they had a son, Oz Perkins, who would go on to become an actor and director.

In 1990, while filming *Psycho IV: The Beginning*, Perkins underwent blood tests after experiencing facial palsy. The results brought a devastating revelation—he was HIV-positive. However, Perkins didn't learn of his diagnosis from a doctor. Instead, the news was leaked to the *National Enquirer*, and he discovered the truth when he saw the tabloid headline while standing in a grocery store checkout line.

On September 12, 1992, Perkins passed away from AIDS-related pneumonia at the age of 60, leaving behind his wife and children. Less than a decade later, tragedy struck again.

On September 11, 2001, Berry Berenson was aboard American Airlines Flight 11 when it was hijacked and crashed into the North Tower of the World Trade Center, making her one of the victims of the 9/11 attacks.

The Perkins family's story, marked by talent, success, and profound loss, remains one of Hollywood's most poignant tragedies.

THE REAL-LIFE FINAL DESTINATION

In 1955, during the grueling 24-hour race at Le Mans, driver Lance Macklin found himself caught in a split-second disaster. As he sped down the track, a competitor ahead of him suddenly braked, forcing Macklin to swerve sharply to avoid a collision. In the chaos, his car was struck at high speed by Pierre Levegh's vehicle, setting off one of the deadliest tragedies in motorsports history.

The impact sent Levegh's car flying through the air at 125 miles per hour. Thrown from the vehicle, Levegh was killed instantly. His airborne car then crashed into the packed grandstands and exploded upon impact. The force of the explosion sent the hood and engine hurtling into the crowd like lethal shrapnel. The car's magnesium bodywork ignited instantly, raining down flames and debris. The hood, slicing through the stands like a massive blade, decapitated several spectators, while others perished in the ensuing fire.

The devastation was unimaginable. A total of 83 people lost their lives, and another 120 were severely injured.

The 1955 Le Mans disaster remains the deadliest accident in racing history, a haunting reminder of the dangers of motorsport and a tragedy that forever changed the landscape of auto racing.

MANSFIELD ON FIRE

Martha Mansfield was born on July 14, 1899, in New York City and quickly became enamored with the rising film industry. In 1920, she secured her most memorable role as Millicent Carew in the 1920 adaptation of *Dr. Jekyll and Mr. Hyde*, starring opposite the legendary John Barrymore. Her captivating performance caught the attention of Hollywood producers, leading her to sign a contract with David O. Selznick and Fox Film Corporation. In 1923, she starred in *The Silent Command* alongside Bela Lugosi, years before he became synonymous with *Dracula*.

Later that year, Mansfield traveled to San Antonio, Texas, to film the Civil War drama *The Warrens of Virginia*. The film's period costumes included heavy, highly flammable hoop skirts, a serious hazard on set—especially in an era when movie safety standards were lax. Though cast and crew were warned about the dangers of open flames near the costumes, disaster struck in the most horrifying way.

After filming a scene, Mansfield sat in the backseat of a car when, without warning, her dress ignited. Her co-star, Wilfred Lytell, desperately tried to smother the flames with his jacket, but the fire spread rapidly. While her face and neck were miraculously spared, the rest of her body suffered severe third-degree burns. Mansfield was rushed to the hospital, but despite efforts to save her, she succumbed to her injuries the following day, on November 30, 1923, at just 24 years old.

The exact cause of the fire remains a mystery. Some speculated it was an accident, while rumors suggested a more sinister possibility—that a disgruntled crew member may have been responsible. In the aftermath, much of Mansfield's footage was removed from the film, marking the tragic and premature end of a promising career.

THE TRAGIC LIFE OF KELSEY GRAMMER

Kelsey Grammer, best known for his role on *Frasier*, was born in 1955 in St. Thomas, Virgin Islands. From an early age, his life was shaped by a series of devastating tragedies. After his parents divorced, he moved to Florida to live with his grandparents. In 1967, the loss of his grandfather marked the first of several heartbreaking events that would follow.

The next year, following the assassination of Martin Luther King Jr., unrest swept through the Virgin Islands. During this period of violence, Grammer's father became a victim. Rioters encircled his home with fire, forcing him outside, where he was fatally shot.

In 1975, at just 20 years old, Grammer endured yet another horrific loss. His younger sister, living in Colorado Springs, was abducted by serial killer Freddie Glenn. She was brutally raped and murdered—a trauma that would haunt Grammer for the rest of his life.

Tragedy struck again five years later when his two half-brothers were killed while scuba diving. It is believed they were attacked by sharks. These deeply personal and harrowing experiences left an indelible mark on Grammer's life, shaping him with resilience and depth. Despite facing unimaginable loss, he went on to become one of television's most celebrated actors, carrying with him a strength forged through pain and perseverance.

GAME NIGHT GONE WRONG

Primmie Niven, an English actress, was married to David Niven, the renowned actor known for his roles in the original *Casino Royale* and *The Pink Panther*. The couple were fixtures in Hollywood's elite social scene during the 1940s, often attending glamorous parties alongside the biggest stars of the era.

On May 19, 1946, the Nivens attended a dinner party at the home of actor Tyrone Power. Among the distinguished guests were Rex Harrison, Cesar Romero, and Oleg Cassini, the future fashion designer for Jackie Kennedy. After dinner, the group decided to play a lighthearted game of hide-and-seek in the dark.

As the game unfolded, a sudden loud thud interrupted the laughter. When the lights were turned on, they discovered Primmie lying at the bottom of a staircase. In the darkness, she had unknowingly opened a basement door and fallen down the steps, landing hard on the concrete floor below.

David Niven and Tyrone Power rushed to her side and carried her to a sofa, where she drifted in and out of consciousness. An ambulance arrived, and she was taken to the hospital, initially showing signs of recovery despite suffering a severe concussion.

Tragically, after undergoing surgery the following evening, her condition took a turn for the worse, and she passed away at just 28 years old. Her shocking and untimely death cast a pall over Hollywood's golden era and left David Niven devastated. What began as an evening of carefree fun ended in heartbreak, marking one of the most tragic accidents in Hollywood history.

BROTHERS, BIKES, AND BACKROADS

On October 29, 1971, just months after the release of *The Allman Brothers Band at Fillmore East*, guitarist Duane Allman was riding his Harley-Davidson motorcycle on a back road in Macon, Georgia. As he approached an intersection, a flatbed truck suddenly stopped in the middle of the road. Attempting to swerve out of the way, Allman lost control and collided with the vehicle. The impact sent him flying, with his motorcycle landing on top of him as he skidded nearly 90 feet down the road.

Rushed to the hospital, Allman underwent emergency treatment, but his internal injuries were too severe. Just a few hours later, he passed away at the age of 24, leaving behind an indelible legacy as one of rock's most gifted guitarists.

Tragically, barely a year later, the Allman Brothers Band suffered another devastating loss. On November 11, 1972, bassist Barry Oakley was also riding his motorcycle when he collided with a bus. Thrown from his bike, Oakley initially refused medical attention and returned home, unaware of the severity of his injuries.

Hours later, he was rushed to the hospital after experiencing intense pain and confusion. Doctors discovered he had suffered a fractured skull, which led to fatal brain swelling. Like Allman, Oakley was just 24 years old when he died.

In a chilling coincidence, his crash occurred less than three blocks from the site of Allman's fatal accident. The loss of both musicians in such eerily similar circumstances cast a haunting shadow over the band's history, forever marking The Allman Brothers Band with a sense of tragedy that would become inseparable from their legend.

JACKIE WILSON AND THE KING

In *1975*, legendary soul and R&B singer Jackie Wilson took the stage for a performance on the *Dick Clark Review*, delivering his electrifying hit "Lonely Teardrops". As he reached the lyric "my heart is crying," Wilson suddenly flipped onto his back. The audience erupted in applause, assuming it was just another one of his signature dramatic stage moves. But it wasn't. At that very moment, Jackie Wilson suffered a massive heart attack at just 41 years old.

Unbeknownst to his fans, Wilson had unknowingly been jeopardizing his own health for years. Believing that audiences loved to see him sweat on stage, he had developed a dangerous pre-show ritual—consuming large amounts of salt tablets and drinking excessive water to enhance his performance. This routine, combined with an already demanding lifestyle, contributed to his declining heart health.

Though he survived the heart attack, Wilson was left severely incapacitated and was ultimately placed in a nursing home, losing everything he had earned. His once-thriving career was over, and he faced financial ruin.

Then, in 1976, Wilson's close friend, Etta James, made a startling discovery. The person quietly covering Wilson's medical bills and nursing home expenses was none other than Elvis Presley.

Presley, who had long admired Wilson's talent, took it upon himself to support the singer without seeking recognition. Even after Elvis's death in 1977, his estate continued paying for Wilson's care until his passing in 1984.

Jackie Wilson's tragic decline is forever intertwined with the quiet generosity of Elvis Presley, a gesture of deep admiration and respect between two musical icons—one that remained largely unknown until years later.

CHAPTER 5

SPORTS LEGENDS

MAD MARTY BERGEN

Marty Bergen was a professional baseball player who served as a catcher for the Boston Bean Eaters from 1896 to 1899—a team that would later become the Atlanta Braves. Widely regarded as one of the best catchers of his era, his defensive skills and athleticism were undeniable. However, his career and legacy remain overshadowed by his erratic behavior and tragic downfall, making his induction into the Hall of Fame unlikely despite past votes in his favor.

Bergen struggled with severe mental health issues that strained his relationships with teammates. He became convinced that some of them were trying to poison him, leading to violent altercations and growing paranoia. His condition worsened in 1899 after the death of his young son, Martin Jr., from diphtheria. When he returned to the team, he imagined that his teammates were mocking his son's passing, though there was no evidence to support his fears. His paranoia intensified—he believed people were throwing knives at him during games, making it nearly impossible for him to continue playing.

By 1900, Bergen's mental state had deteriorated beyond control. On January 19 of that year, neighbors visited his home and found him in an unusually cheerful mood, enjoying their company. But shortly after, he committed an unthinkable act. In a violent episode, Bergen murdered his wife and two young children with an axe before taking his own life by slitting his throat with a razor blade. He was just 28 years old.

Despite his undeniable talent, Marty Bergen's career remains overshadowed by his tragic struggle with mental illness—a chilling reminder of the darkness that can lurk behind even the brightest athletic talent.

ARMY-NAVY GAME, ARMY-NAVY GAME

The Army-Navy game is one of college football's most anticipated matchups, drawing millions of viewers each year. One of the most memorable moments in the sport's history took place during the 1963 game, forever changing the way football is broadcast.

On December 7, 1963, Army quarterback Rollie Stichweh appeared to score two one-yard touchdowns in rapid succession, leaving viewers baffled. The confusion wasn't due to a rule change or a miscall—it was the first-ever use of instant replay on live television. The groundbreaking technology, introduced by CBS, was so unfamiliar that many viewers thought the network had made an error in their broadcast. Complaints flooded in, prompting CBS to discontinue its use for the remainder of the game. Despite the initial skepticism, instant replay would go on to revolutionize sports broadcasting.

However, the emotional weight of the 1963 game extended far beyond the innovation on-screen. President John F. Kennedy, a devoted Navy football fan, had been scheduled to attend and perform the coin toss.

Tragically, just weeks before the game, he was assassinated in Dallas. In his honor, the game was rescheduled to December 7—the anniversary of Pearl Harbor. With heavy hearts, the teams took the field, and Navy secured a 21-15 victory in front of a grieving nation. The stadium where the game was played would later be renamed John F. Kennedy Stadium, further cementing its place in history.

Adding another layer of coincidence, the *Life* magazine issue released following Kennedy's assassination, featuring the president on its cover, was not the original choice for that issue. The person who was supposed to grace the cover of *Life* magazine for that issue was Roger Staubach, the quarterback for that Navy team. Staubach would go on to achieve legendary status, winning two Super Bowls with the Dallas Cowboys, the NFL team based in the same city where Kennedy was assassinated.

THE MAJOR LEAGUE SPY

Moe Berg was one of the most intriguing figures in Major League Baseball history—a catcher whose career spanned from 1923 to 1939, yet his legacy extends far beyond the sport. Not only was he a skilled player, but he was also a brilliant intellect, widely regarded as a certified genius.

In 1934, Berg joined a goodwill baseball tour to Japan alongside legends like Babe Ruth and Lou Gehrig. While the trip was meant to foster international relations, Berg had an agenda of his own. Armed with a home movie camera, he filmed Tokyo's skyline and key military installations from the rooftop of a hospital, capturing footage that would later prove invaluable. Upon his return to the United States, the government took a keen interest in his recordings. Recognizing his intellect and resourcefulness, officials recruited him as a spy.

His most critical mission came during World War II when he was sent to Switzerland to attend a lecture by German physicist Werner Heisenberg. His objective was to assess Germany's progress in developing an atomic bomb.

If Heisenberg appeared to be close to completing the weapon, Berg had direct orders to assassinate him on the spot.

Moe Berg's life was a rare fusion of athletics, intelligence, and espionage, making him one of the most enigmatic figures in both baseball and covert operations. His story remains one of the most extraordinary in the history of sports—and international intrigue.

A LEGEND ON AND OFF THE COURT

Norris Williams, the top-ranked U.S. tennis player in 1916, overcame unimaginable adversity to achieve greatness. In April 1912, he and his father were passengers aboard the *Titanic*, returning to the United States from Ireland. When the ship struck an iceberg and began its tragic descent, the pair remained onboard until the final moments before leaping into the freezing Atlantic.

Amid the chaos, one of the ship's towering smokestacks collapsed, killing Williams' father instantly. Norris, however, managed to swim to a lifeboat, where he endured hours knee-deep in the frigid water before being rescued. The extreme cold caused severe frostbite in his legs, and doctors recommended amputation. Refusing to accept that fate, Williams was determined to recover. He forced himself to walk constantly to restore circulation—an unconventional and painful method that, against all odds, saved his legs.Not only did he fully recover, but he returned to tennis and reached the pinnacle of the sport.

In addition to becoming the No. 1 player in the U.S. in 1916, he also won an Olympic gold medal 12 years after surviving the *Titanic* disaster. His story is a testament to extraordinary resilience and determination, proving that his indomitable spirit was just as formidable as his talent on the court.

A DIAMOND DEBUT

On October 2, 1977, during the Los Angeles Dodgers' final regular-season game against the Houston Astros, outfielder Dusty Baker stepped up to the plate and crushed his 30th home run of the season. As he rounded the bases and approached the on-deck circle, his teammate Glenn Burke stood waiting to congratulate him. In a spontaneous moment, Burke lifted his hand in celebration. Without thinking, Baker instinctively raised his own hand and smacked it against Burke's. In that instant, the high five was born.

What seemed like a simple act of joy between teammates would go on to become one of the most universally recognized gestures of celebration. But its story didn't end there.

Glenn Burke would later become one of the first openly gay players in Major League Baseball. After retiring at just 27 years old, he embraced the high five as a symbol of pride while living in San Francisco's Castro District, giving the gesture a deeper cultural meaning beyond sports.

Meanwhile, Dusty Baker continued to make baseball history. Having been on deck when Hank Aaron shattered Babe Ruth's record with his 715th home run, Baker went on to become one of the game's most respected managers. In 2022, he led the Houston Astros to a World Series victory, cementing his legacy in the sport.

What began as a spontaneous moment on a baseball diamond evolved into a global symbol of excitement, unity, and triumph. The high five, born in the heat of competition, transcended sports to carry a legacy that spans both athletic achievement and LGBTQ+ pride, proving that even the smallest moments can leave an enduring impact on history.

THE WORLD'S GREATEST ATHELETE

In 1904, 16-year-old Native American Jim Thorpe moved to Pennsylvania to live with his father. One day, while walking home from work, he passed his high school and noticed the track and field team practicing the high jump. Curious, he asked if he could give it a try. Hoping to humiliate him, the boys on the team set the bar at 5'9"—the school record at the time. To their shock, Thorpe, still dressed in his work clothes and heavy boots, cleared the bar on his first attempt.

His extraordinary athleticism caught the attention of one of the school's coaches—Glenn "Pop" Warner, who would later become a legendary figure in American football. Warner personally took Thorpe under his wing, helping to shape his athletic career.

By 1907, Thorpe was playing football at Carlisle Indian Industrial School. In a game against the West Point Army team, he scored a remarkable 96-yard touchdown—only to have it nullified by a penalty. Undeterred, on the very next play, he ran for a 97-yard touchdown, leaving the crowd in awe. One of the West Point players he faced that day was Dwight D. Eisenhower, the future President of the United States.

In 1912, Thorpe competed in the Summer Olympics, excelling in the pentathlon, decathlon, and even the javelin throw—a sport he had never attempted before. Unaware that a running start was allowed, he threw from a stationary position and still managed to win a bronze medal.

Before the decathlon, Thorpe's shoes were stolen. Determined to compete, he found a mismatched pair in a trash can—one too big and the other too small. Adjusting the larger shoe with extra socks, he powered through the event and won the gold medal in the decathlon, cementing his place as one of the world's greatest athletes.

Three years later, in 1915, Thorpe began playing professional football for the Canton Bulldogs, where he also served as the team's coach until 1920. His success and star power with the Bulldogs were so influential that they helped inspire the creation of the Pro Football Hall of Fame in Canton, Ohio. Even after retiring from football at 41, Thorpe continued his athletic career, playing professional basketball and baseball.

His unparalleled versatility and determination solidified his legacy as one of the greatest all-around athletes in history. Jim Thorpe's extraordinary feats and unwavering spirit continue to inspire generations, proving that true greatness knows no bounds.

RUBE THE RECKLESS

Rube Waddell was one of Major League Baseball's most talented yet eccentric pitchers, playing for teams like the Pittsburgh Pirates and the Chicago Orphans over a 13-year career. While his skills on the mound were undeniable, Waddell became just as famous—if not more so—for his bizarre and unpredictable behavior.

Known for his short attention span, he was easily distracted mid-game, once abandoning the field to chase a passing fire truck. On another occasion, he abruptly left a game to go fishing. His offseason antics were equally strange—he would often disappear for weeks at a time, only for teammates to later discover he had joined a traveling circus or was wrestling alligators for sport.

Despite his quirks, Waddell had a deeply compassionate side. In 1913, while playing in Kentucky, he volunteered to help rescue victims of a catastrophic flood, wading through freezing waters for days to bring people to safety. Unfortunately, his heroism had dire consequences—he contracted pneumonia twice, which later developed into tuberculosis. The illness ultimately took his life in 1914 at just 37 years old.

Rube Waddell's legacy is one of both remarkable athleticism and outlandish antics, making him one of baseball's most unforgettable characters.

LISTON'S LEGACY

Sonny Liston was the 24th of 25 children, though his exact birth date remains uncertain, with estimates placing it between 1928 and 1935. Raised in extreme poverty, he left school at a young age to help support his family. One of his early jobs involved working as a debt collector for the mafia, where his brutal enforcement tactics often left debtors battered and broken—a level of violence that would later define his career in the boxing ring.

Liston rose to prominence as one of the most intimidating heavyweight boxers in history. His sheer power and relentless aggression made him a formidable opponent, striking fear into even the toughest fighters. Muhammad Ali once admitted that the only time he ever felt true fear in the ring was when he faced Sonny Liston.

After his boxing career ended, Liston settled in Las Vegas, where he reportedly resumed his work as a mafia enforcer—a move that put him in dangerous circles. On January 5, 1971, at the age of 38, Liston was found dead in his home by his wife, Geraldine.

The official cause of death was listed as heart failure, but the discovery of needle marks on his arm fueled widespread speculation that he had been murdered, possibly as a result of his connections to the Las Vegas underworld.

To this day, the circumstances surrounding Liston's death remain shrouded in mystery, leaving behind a legacy of dominance in the ring and unanswered questions outside of it.

CHAPTER 6

SEXS, DRUGS, AND ROCK N' ROLL

BATMAN: THE WORLD'S GREATEST LOVER

Actor Adam West became a household name in the 1960s for his portrayal of Batman, the caped crusader of Gotham. However, off-screen, he became equally notorious in Hollywood for his extravagant and unapologetic lifestyle. Known for his endless charm and playboy antics, West reportedly had affairs with up to eight women a day, including Hollywood icons Natalie Wood and Raquel Welch.

His reputation for indulgence reached such heights that after a particularly eventful stay in Aspen, Colorado—where he allegedly seduced a large number of the city's female population—the city banned him from returning for 15 years. On the set of *Batman*, his escapades continued, with West frequently engaging in trysts between scenes, during lunch breaks, and at nearly every available opportunity. At times, a literal queue of admirers would form outside his dressing room, waiting for their chance to spend time with the star.

One of the most infamous stories of West's wild lifestyle involved his *Batman* co-star Frank Gorshin, who played the Riddler. The two actors once attended an orgy together but were swiftly asked to leave—not for their participation, but because they couldn't resist staying in character. Their animated performances, complete with Batman-themed sound effects, proved to be too much for the other guests, cementing their night as one of Hollywood's most bizarre tales of debauchery.

ROCKET MANHOOD

Cary Grant, the legendary star of *North by Northwest*, battled depression for much of his life, trying various treatments with little success. Desperate for relief, he became intrigued by the work of Dr. Timothy Leary, a California psychologist who had been using LSD to treat mental health disorders with remarkable results. Inspired by Leary's findings, Grant sought out Dr. Mortimer Hartman at the Psychiatric Institute of Beverly Hills, where he began a series of guided LSD therapy sessions. Under Hartman's supervision, Grant would take the drug and undergo structured "trips," during which his visions were analyzed in hopes of uncovering the root of his emotional struggles.

One of Grant's most bizarre hallucinations involved seeing himself as a giant, penis-shaped rocket, launching from Earth into deep space. Over time, Grant underwent more than 100 LSD sessions, crediting the psychedelic experience with transforming his mental state and even saving his life.

Once known for his reserved and stoic demeanor, he became an outspoken advocate for the drug, openly praising its therapeutic benefits at a time when mental health—and especially its treatment—was rarely discussed in public, let alone by a major Hollywood star.

In 1966, Grant retired from acting—the same year LSD was made illegal in the United States. As the drug became synonymous with the growing counterculture movement of the late 1960s, Grant's endorsement of it began to wane.

The chaotic and rebellious image of psychedelics clashed with his more structured, therapeutic experience, leading him to distance himself from the movement. However, despite his eventual retreat from advocacy, Grant remains one of the first, if not *the* first, celebrity to publicly embrace psychedelics—forever cementing his legacy as an unlikely pioneer in the discussion of mental health treatment.

A MONSTEROUS MUSE

Cathy Smith was a Canadian woman whose life was deeply intertwined with the rock and roll scene, as well as a long battle with drug addiction. While in Canada, she became close with Levon Helm, the drummer for The Band, a legendary rock group that first gained fame as Bob Dylan's backing band. However, after a major falling out with The Band, Smith moved on to another renowned Canadian musician, Gordon Lightfoot. Their turbulent relationship reportedly inspired Lightfoot's classic hit *Sundown*, a song believed to reflect his jealousy and concern over Smith's self-destructive lifestyle.

Throughout the 1970s, Cathy Smith made a name for herself in the rock and roll scene as a backup singer for musician Hoyt Axton, the son of Mae Boren, who co-wrote Elvis Presley's 1956 hit song *Heartbreak Hotel*. Smith also briefly served as a drug dealer for Rolling Stones guitarists Ron Wood and Keith Richards. Eventually, Smith relocated to Los Angeles, where she reconnected with members of The Band. In 1976, she accompanied them to New York when they were invited to perform on *Saturday Night Live*.

During this time, she crossed paths with John Belushi, a rising comedy icon and cast member of the show.

On March 5, 1982, Belushi called Smith and invited her to his bungalow at the Chateau Marmont in Los Angeles. That night, actor Robin Williams briefly stopped by but quickly left, later admitting he felt "creeped out" by Smith's presence.

After Williams' departure, Smith injected Belushi with a lethal combination of heroin and cocaine, commonly known as a "speedball." Just hours later, the *Saturday Night Live* star and *Blues Brothers* frontman was found dead at only 33 years old.

THE LADIES MAN?

On October 18, 1974, soul singer Al Green was at home with his girlfriend, Mary Woodson, discussing their relationship. Mary wanted to get married, but Green did not share her desire for commitment.

Shortly after he excused himself to the bathroom, Mary entered with a pot of boiling grits and poured it over him, causing severe burns that required skin grafts on his stomach, back, and arms. Immediately after the attack, she went into another room, grabbed a .38 revolver, and took her own life.

As if that ordeal weren't shocking enough, just days after Green was discharged from the hospital, his female cousin arrived at his home and held him hostage at gunpoint.

However, Green's troubled history with women suggests his misfortunes may not have been entirely unwarranted. His first wife later alleged that in 1978, while she was five months pregnant, he struck her over the head with a boot.

That same year, he reportedly beat another woman with a large tree limb. In 1974—the same year of the boiling grits incident—he also pushed his secretary through a glass door after refusing to pay her money he owed.

Despite his legendary status in soul music, Green's personal life was riddled with violence, turmoil, and controversy, leaving behind a legacy as troubled as it was influential.

A SLICK TRICK ON TRICKY DICK

During Richard Nixon's presidency, his daughter Tricia attended Finch College, a prestigious school for women. Wanting to honor its alumni, Nixon decided to host a White House reception, inviting former students to attend. Among those invited was a young woman named Grace Wing. However, by the time the invitation reached her, she had undergone a radical transformation—no longer just another Finch College alumna, she was now *Grace Slick*, the lead singer of Jefferson Airplane and a symbol of the very counterculture Nixon despised.

This invitation presented a unique opportunity for Grace, who harbored deep resentment toward Nixon, whom the counterculture blamed for the Vietnam War's escalation and his administration's staunch anti-drug policies. Rather than politely attending, she devised a plan to make the event *far* more memorable. She decided to bring activist Abbie Hoffman—a leader of the Yippie movement and one of Nixon's most vocal critics—as her plus-one. Together, they plotted to spike the president's tea with 600 micrograms of LSD, an act that would have been one of the most infamous pranks in political history.

Their plan, however, was thwarted by an unexpected technicality—the reception was strictly for women. As soon as Hoffman arrived, his unmistakable presence raised suspicion, and security immediately denied him entry. Without her co-conspirator, Grace abandoned the event altogether, leaving Nixon's tea untouched and ensuring that the plot never came to fruition.

Though her plan to dose the president failed, the mere fact that she nearly pulled it off remains one of the most bizarre "what if" moments in White House history.

THE KILLER

Jerry Lee Lewis, a rock and roll pioneer, lived a life as wild as his music, marked by seven marriages and a string of controversies. His most infamous union came at the age of 22 when he married his 13-year-old cousin, Myra Gale Brown. Their scandalous relationship shocked the public, especially after Myra gave birth to their first child at just 14 years old. Years later, his seventh marriage also stirred controversy—this time to Judith Brown, the ex-wife of Myra's brother, making her yet another cousin by marriage.

While Lewis was celebrated for his electrifying stage presence, earning him the nickname "The Killer," his offstage antics were just as notorious. In 1983, his fifth wife, Shawn Stephens, died under suspicious circumstances, reportedly from a methadone overdose. However, troubling details emerged—her body was allegedly covered in blood and bruises, leading to speculation about foul play. Though Lewis was never charged, doubts about the nature of her death persisted. His reckless behavior wasn't limited to his personal relationships.

As a young man, Lewis was involved in a violent altercation where he attempted to strangle another boy during a fight. In 1976, while carelessly handling a .357 Magnum, he accidentally shot his bass player in the chest. Miraculously, the musician survived. Later that same year, in a drunken haze, Lewis crashed his car into the gates of Graceland, brandishing a gun and demanding to confront Elvis Presley over who truly deserved the title of "The King." Elvis, wisely avoiding the confrontation, stayed inside while Lewis was arrested.

Despite his many scandals, Jerry Lee Lewis remained one of rock and roll's most influential figures—a legend whose talent was as undeniable as his infamy.

THE FBI AND THE ROCK N ROLL CLASSIC

When The Kingsmen released their version of "Louie Louie" in 1963, it became an instant sensation, climbing to #2 on the Billboard charts. The song's slurred, nearly indecipherable lyrics sparked curiosity—and controversy. Indiana Governor Matthew Welsh claimed the lyrics were obscene, stating they made his "ears tingle" upon hearing them. He filed a formal complaint with the FCC, but after reviewing the track, the agency determined the lyrics were too unintelligible to be deemed offensive.

The controversy escalated to the point where Attorney General Robert F. Kennedy got involved, leading to an FBI investigation into the song's content. After months of scrutiny and extensive analysis, the FBI ultimately concluded that the lyrics were incomprehensible and found no evidence of obscenity.

Ironically, amid all the outrage and government scrutiny, no one noticed a real slip-up hidden in the recording. At the 54-second mark, the drummer accidentally dropped his drumstick and audibly muttered *"fuck."*

The unintended expletive went completely unnoticed by censors and investigators alike, adding an unexpected twist to the song's already notorious history.

This bizarre chapter only cemented "Louie Louie's" place in rock 'n' roll legend—a simple, garbled tune that ignited a cultural firestorm, baffled the authorities, and endured as a rebellious anthem for generations.

THE ROCK N ROLL GENE

Gene Vincent was a rockabilly trailblazer, often regarded as a wilder, more rebellious counterpart to Elvis Presley. His 1956 hit "Be-Bop-A-Lula" launched him into stardom, making him one of the defining figures of early rock 'n' roll. With his signature sneer, raw energy, and unpredictable stage presence, Vincent became a sensation, particularly in Europe, where he toured extensively.

However, his life took a tragic turn on April 16, 1960, while traveling through England with fellow rock star Eddie Cochran. Their car was involved in a catastrophic accident, leaving Vincent badly injured. Cochran, just 21 years old, was thrown from the vehicle and died the following day.

By chance, musician Tony Sheridan had considered joining them that night but decided against it. Had he got in the vehicle that day he very well may have perished alongside Cochran. This means that he would never have been able to travel to Hamburg, Germany a few years later, where he became a mentor to up-and-coming bands—including a young group from Liverpool that would later be known as *The Beatles*.

Vincent's later years were plagued by personal demons. Struggling with alcoholism and an explosive temper, he became infamous for his erratic behavior, often carrying a gun. He once brandished a firearm at his girlfriend in front of a young Paul McCartney and, during a heated hotel argument, fired a shot at musician Paul Raven—who would later gain notoriety as Gary Glitter. He even threatened The Doors drummer John Densmore with a gun.

Despite his immense talent and influence, Vincent's career spiraled downward. His reckless lifestyle and declining health took their toll, and in 1971, at just 36 years old, he died from a hemorrhage and heart failure. Though his life was marked by chaos, his music left an indelible impact on rock 'n' roll, securing his place as both a pioneer and a cautionary tale of the genre's excesses.

FOGERTY VS FOGERTY

In 1970, legendary rock band Creedence Clearwater Revival (CCR) released "Run Through the Jungle," a song written by their frontman, John Fogerty. Just two years later, CCR disbanded, and their record label, Fantasy Records, took ownership of the band's entire catalog. Despite this, Fogerty pressed on with his solo career, achieving significant success.

In 1985, Fogerty released "The Old Man Down the Road," a song with a melody strikingly similar to "Run Through the Jungle." Almost immediately, Fantasy Records filed a lawsuit, accusing Fogerty of copyright infringement—ironically, for writing a song that sounded too much like one of his own past compositions.

The case escalated to the Supreme Court, where Fogerty defended his right to create music in his own style. In a landmark ruling, the Court sided with him, affirming that an artist cannot be sued for resembling their own previous work. This victory not only upheld Fogerty's creative freedom but also set a crucial legal precedent in music copyright law, protecting artists from being penalized for their signature sound.

THE DAY THE MUSIC DIED

In early 1959, rock and roll pioneer Buddy Holly embarked on the *Winter Dance Party* tour alongside his band, The Crickets—then featuring Tommy Allsup, Carl Bunch, and a young Waylon Jennings, who would later become a country music legend. Joining them on the tour were rising stars Ritchie Valens and The Big Bopper. The tour's schedule was relentless, forcing the musicians to endure long, freezing journeys across the northern United States in an unheated bus.

By February 2, 1959, exhaustion and harsh conditions had taken their toll. That night, a small charter plane became available, offering a few musicians a chance to avoid another grueling bus ride. However, with limited seats, who would board was decided through coin flips and seat swaps. Tommy Allsup flipped a coin with Ritchie Valens, who won and, unaware of his fate, cheerfully remarked, "That's the first thing I've ever won in my entire life." Meanwhile, Waylon Jennings gave up his seat to The Big Bopper, who was suffering from the flu.

Before parting, Buddy Holly jokingly told Jennings, "I hope your bus freezes up." In a playful response, Jennings quipped, "I hope your damn plane crashes." Hours later, at 1:00 a.m. on February 3, 1959, tragedy struck. The plane crashed into an Iowa field, killing everyone on board instantly. Buddy Holly was just 22 years old, Ritchie Valens only 17, and The Big Bopper 28. The loss of these young stars left an indelible mark on music history, later memorialized as *The Day the Music Died*.

CHAPTER 7

BAD BEHAVIOR

BOBBY'S BETRAYAL

Bobby Womack, a soul singer from Cleveland, Ohio, gained fame with his hit song *Across 110th Street*, but his musical journey began long before that. He first performed with his brothers in a gospel group that later transitioned into R&B, becoming known as The Womack Brothers. Their talent caught the attention of soul legend Sam Cooke, who became their mentor and helped secure their first record deal in the early 1960s, launching Womack's path to success.

Tragedy struck in 1964 when Cooke was shot and killed under controversial circumstances. The loss of his friend and mentor deeply affected Womack, but his ties to Cooke's life didn't end there. Less than three months after Cooke's death, Womack began a relationship with Barbara Cooke, Sam's widow. Their romance quickly led to marriage, and in a striking and controversial move, Womack arrived at the courthouse wearing one of Sam Cooke's suits.

The marriage lasted only four years before ending in scandal. Barbara discovered Womack was having an affair, but the revelation became even more shocking when it was revealed that his mistress was Linda Cooke—
Sam Cooke's teenage daughter and Womack's own stepdaughter.

MOMMY MURDER

Jim Gordon was one of the most prolific rock drummers of the 1970s. His career took off with contributions to the Beach Boys' legendary album *Pet Sounds*, showcasing his exceptional talent. He later joined Eric Clapton's band, Derek and the Dominos, helping to craft their iconic hit "Layla." The song's unforgettable piano coda, often considered one of rock's greatest musical moments, was remarkably composed by Gordon himself.

Despite his success, Gordon's life took a dark and tragic turn. He began suffering from severe paranoid delusions, later attributed to undiagnosed schizophrenia. The voices haunting him, he believed, were those of his mother. Desperate to silence them, he committed an unthinkable act.

On the night of June 3, 1983, Gordon drove to his mother's home while she slept. In a brutal attack, he struck her repeatedly with a hammer before stabbing her to death with a butcher knife. He was arrested soon after and charged with her murder.

During his trial, Gordon was diagnosed with schizophrenia, yet despite his mental illness, he was sentenced to life in prison. He remained incarcerated for the rest of his life, passing away in 2023. Once celebrated as one of rock and roll's greatest drummers, his legacy is now forever overshadowed by the devastating effects of untreated mental illness and the horrific crime that defined his later years.

FUN AND GAMES WITH ALFRED HITCHCOCK

Alfred Hitchcock's childhood was steeped in loneliness, fear, and severe beatings—both at home and at school. These early experiences of terror profoundly shaped his filmmaking, giving him an unparalleled ability to evoke fear on screen. They also contributed to the darker, more controversial aspects of his private life.

Hitchcock was known for his eccentric dinner parties, where he would serve elaborate multi-course meals, all dyed the same color—most famously, blue. He never explained the bizarre theme, adding to his reputation as a mischievous prankster. However, his pranks often took a much darker turn.

One of his most infamous stunts involved a cruel bet with a film crew member. Hitchcock and the man wagered that he couldn't spend the night handcuffed to a camera rig at the studio. To raise the stakes, Hitchcock, unbeknownst to the crew member, laced the man's brandy with a powerful laxative. By morning, the crew member was found in a wretched state—sobbing, exhausted, and covered in his own filth.

While the rest of the crew was horrified, Hitchcock reportedly found the ordeal hilarious.

His love of pranks extended to his actresses, frequently exploiting their fears for his own amusement. He once locked actress Elsie Randolph inside a smoke-filled phone booth, fully aware that it was her greatest fear.

However, his cruelest behavior was reserved for Tippi Hedren during the making of *The Birds*. In the film's harrowing attack scene, Hitchcock subjected her to real birds rather than the mechanical ones she had expected, inflicting both physical injuries and deep emotional trauma. His torment didn't stop when filming ended—he later sent her young daughter, Melanie Griffith, a disturbing "gift": a wax figure of Hedren lying in a coffin.

While Hitchcock's brilliance made him one of the most influential filmmakers in history, his sadistic tendencies left behind a legacy as unsettling as the films he created.

AVA'S AFFAIRS

Despite her success on screen, Ava Gardner's personal life was filled with tumultuous relationships and fiery romances. She married child star Mickey Rooney in 1942, but the union quickly crumbled when he had an affair while she was recovering from surgery. Not long after, she entered a stormy relationship with aviation mogul Howard Hughes—so volatile that, in a fit of rage, she once hurled an ashtray at him with enough force to nearly kill him.

Her second marriage, to bandleader Artie Shaw, was equally short-lived. During this time, she also had an affair with director John Huston. However, it was her third marriage, to Frank Sinatra from 1951 to 1957, that became the stuff of Hollywood legend. Their relationship was a whirlwind of passion, drama, and reckless escapades—including wild nights in Palm Springs where they would drive around shooting out streetlights. Yet even amid the chaos, Gardner had an affair with actor Robert Mitchum.

After their divorce, she didn't hold back when commenting on Sinatra's next marriage to actress Mia Farrow, famously remarking, *"I always knew Frank would end up in bed with a boy."*

In her later years, Gardner relocated to Spain, where she befriended Ernest Hemingway and even lived with him for a time. After his death in 1961, she moved to London, where, in 1986, a stroke left her partially paralyzed. On January 25, 1990, at the age of 67, she passed away from pneumonia and fibrosis, leaving behind a legacy as one of Hollywood's most captivating and untamed stars.

STRANGER THAN FICTION

In 1935, Universal Pictures released *Life Returns*, a film inspired by the controversial experiments of Dr. Robert Cornish. The movie featured real footage of a dead dog being brought back to life—an actual experiment conducted by Cornish himself. Using a combination of adrenaline and anticoagulants, he had successfully revived two dogs, a process that director Eugene Frenke captured on film. Marketed as a shocking "freakshow" spectacle, the film sparked immediate outrage. Following a disastrous premiere, where horrified audiences and protestors condemned it, *Life Returns* was swiftly pulled from distribution.

Despite the backlash, Cornish remained undeterred and set his sights on an even more ambitious goal—human resurrection. A death row inmate at San Quentin Prison volunteered his body for the experiment after his execution, hoping to be the first person revived under Cornish's method. However, legal complications arose. If Cornish successfully brought the prisoner back to life, he would technically be a living person once again, which could force his release. Concerned officials intervened, effectively shutting down Cornish's efforts to apply his experiments to humans.

With his ambitions thwarted by the law, Cornish's work remained confined to animal experimentation, leaving his controversial legacy as one of science's most unsettling what-ifs.

SEAN IN THE SLAMMER

Sean Penn was immersed in Hollywood from an early age, growing up with his father, Leo Penn, who was deeply involved in the film industry. While attending Santa Monica High School, he shared classrooms with future stars Robert Downey Jr., Charlie Sheen, and Emilio Estevez. His breakout role came in 1982 when he played the iconic stoner Jeff Spicoli in *Fast Times at Ridgemont High*, a performance that made him an instant pop culture sensation.

By 1985, Penn's personal life was making just as many headlines as his career. That year, he began a highly publicized and volatile relationship with Madonna, whom he married in 1986. However, his aggressive behavior soon overshadowed their romance. In 1985, he assaulted a journalist, and the following year, he was involved in two violent incidents, including one where he and his assistant reportedly dangled a man over a ninth-story balcony.

In 1987, while filming *Colors* with Robert Duvall, Penn assaulted an extra, Jeffrey Klein, leading to a reckless driving charge and a 60-day jail sentence.

While behind bars, he received an unsettling letter from one of America's most infamous criminals, signing the letter with a pentagram and urging him to *"stay tough."* That fellow inmate was none other than the Night Stalker Richard Ramirez, the convicted serial killer known for his brutal murder spree across Los Angeles. Unfazed, Penn responded with a harsh and unsympathetic reply, making it clear he had no admiration for Ramirez and even expressing his hope that the killer would die in the gas chamber.

Despite the public controversies, Penn's legacy as a talented actor and a controversial personality remains a defining aspect of his career, illustrating the fine line between fame and notoriety in the spotlight. His encounters with the law and notorious figures like Richard Ramirez have only further cemented his reputation as a complex and, at times, volatile figure.

A KING KIDNAPPED

In 1969, a group of Morehouse College students staged a daring protest against the administration, voicing their frustrations over the way the institution was being run. In a bold act of defiance, they locked members of the school's board of trustees in a room, effectively holding them hostage until their demands for change were met. After intense negotiations, the board ultimately agreed to implement reforms.

However, the victory came at a steep cost for the student protesters. In the aftermath, all participants were expelled from Morehouse—including a young Samuel L. Jackson, who would go on to become one of Hollywood's most legendary actors.

In an ironic twist, one of the board members Jackson helped detain was Martin Luther King Sr., the father of Dr. Martin Luther King Jr., who had been assassinated just a year earlier. Coincidentally, Jackson had actually served as an usher at Dr. King's funeral, unknowingly standing at the crossroads of two pivotal moments—one that honored the civil rights leader's legacy and another that defied authority in the pursuit of justice.

THE BIZARRE BIRTH OF PUNK ROCK

On October 27, 1967, Jim Morrison and The Doors took the stage at the University of Michigan for what should have been an electrifying rock performance. Instead, it spiraled into absolute chaos.

Before the show, the band decided to stop for ice cream—a plan Morrison scoffed at, declaring, "Ice cream is for babies. I want whiskey." True to his word, he downed an entire bottle before stepping on stage. When he finally appeared, he was visibly intoxicated, stumbling through songs and singing in an absurdly high-pitched voice, leaving the audience bewildered. As frustration grew among the crowd, Morrison responded with insults, further butchering the performance. After less than 20 minutes, he had to be carried off stage, triggering a full-scale riot inside the venue.

While most of the audience was outraged, one young spectator saw something different—James Osterberg, a local musician and frontman of The Iguanas. Rather than seeing a disaster, he saw a blueprint for something new.

Inspired by Morrison's raw, reckless stage presence, Osterberg—soon to be known as Iggy Pop—would go on to form The Stooges, pushing the boundaries of punk rock and cementing his reputation as one of the most dangerous frontmen in music history. A show that ended in chaos ultimately sparked a revolution.

Iggy Pop would later create wild stories of his own. During a 1973 performance, while heavily under the influence of drugs, he suddenly became convinced that a gorilla was charging toward him, sending him into a panic. As the figure got closer, he realized it wasn't an animal—it was a man in a gorilla suit. But before he could react, the costumed figure grabbed him, hoisted him into the air, and carried him across the stage. As the crowd roared, the gorilla finally removed its mask—revealing none other than Elton John.

By 1975, Iggy's cocaine addiction had spiraled out of control, leading to his involuntary commitment at a Los Angeles mental institution. But even rehab couldn't stop his legendary antics. A few days after his arrival, two friends, concerned he might be running low on drugs, devised a plan to sneak in and visit him.

Wearing full space suits, they bypassed security undetected, entered Iggy's room, and casually did cocaine with him before slipping away. The nurses, too starstruck to intervene, never questioned their presence.

Those two friends? Dennis Hopper and David Bowie.
From Morrison's drunken debacle to Iggy's punk rock revolution, and from hallucinated gorillas to intergalactic drug deliveries, few artists have lived a life as surreal—and as groundbreaking—as Iggy Pop.

THE DISNEY DEATH-FEST

When we think of classic Walt Disney films, we often picture a mix of heartwarming moments and tales of the extraordinary. During the 1950s, Disney's animated features had become massively successful, so the company decided to venture into the world of documentary filmmaking. In 1958, Walt Disney Productions released *White Wilderness*, a groundbreaking documentary showcasing the harsh, icy landscapes of the Arctic. Lauded for its breathtaking cinematography and depiction of the natural world, the film earned an Academy Award for Best Documentary Feature.

One of its most unforgettable and tragic scenes depicted lemmings—small, fluffy rodents—plunging en masse off a cliff, seemingly engaging in mass suicide as they attempted to cross the Arctic Ocean. The haunting imagery left a lasting impact, reinforcing the idea that nature could be as cruel as it was beautiful. However, there was a major problem: the scene was entirely fabricated.

In the 1980s, an investigation uncovered the disturbing truth. The lemmings had not willingly jumped to their deaths; they had been forced. The film crew used a rotating turntable to disorient the animals before driving them off the cliff. What was presented as a dramatic natural event was, in reality, a staged spectacle—an orchestrated tragedy rather than an act of instinct.

This revelation cast a dark shadow over Disney's reputation, exposing the deceptive tactics used in one of its most celebrated documentaries. What had been accepted as a raw, unfiltered look at nature was, in fact, an illusion, forever tarnishing *White Wilderness* and its legacy.

CHAPTER 8

THE STORY BEHIND THE STORY

THREESOMES, BONDAGE, AND COMIC BOOKS?

In the 1930s, psychologist William Marston and his wife Elizabeth engaged in a passionate argument during which Elizabeth noted that her blood pressure increased when she became angry. She shared this observation with William, proposing a connection between emotional states and blood pressure—a spark that eventually led them to develop an early precursor to the lie detector machine.

At that time, the Marstons were involved in a polyamorous relationship with one of William's former students, Olive Byrne. The trio lived a progressive lifestyle, deeply immersed in various unconventional interests, including an affinity for bondage, which subtly influenced both their personal lives and professional work.

By 1940, Marston, a fervent comic book enthusiast, decided to channel his interest in strong female characters and the dynamics of his unique relationship into creating a revolutionary superhero. Inspired by both Elizabeth and Olive, he brought to life a heroine who symbolized empowerment and justice, armed with a magical lasso that compelled truth-telling—a clear nod to his work on lie detection.

The character made her debut in *All-Star Comics* #8 in December 1941 as Wonder Woman, quickly capturing the public's imagination.

With her iconic lasso of truth and unwavering commitment to justice, Wonder Woman not only became a cultural phenomenon but also a lasting emblem of feminist strength and independence, deeply rooted in the Marstons' exploration of psychology and the complexities of human relationships.

The Story Behind the Story

A NIGHTMARE ORIGIN STORY

During the Vietnam War, the CIA recruited many young men from Southeast Asia—particularly from the Hmong community—to serve alongside U.S. forces in their fight against the North Vietnamese. When the war ended, the Hmong faced severe persecution from the new political regime, forcing thousands to flee to the United States in the 1970s to escape violence and oppression.

Shortly after their arrival, a disturbing and unexplained phenomenon began to unfold. Over the next several years, more than a hundred Hmong men, all seemingly healthy, died in their sleep without any prior medical issues. These deaths were attributed to *Sudden Unexplained Nocturnal Death Syndrome* (SUNDS), a mysterious condition in which victims succumbed to an unknown force while sleeping. Despite medical investigations, no definitive explanation has ever been found for the chilling pattern of fatalities.

The wave of unexplained deaths soon became a national news story, drawing widespread attention after a series of articles in the *Los Angeles Times*.

One of the readers captivated by this eerie mystery was a young filmmaker named Wes Craven. Intrigued by the terrifying idea of dying in one's sleep, Craven used it as inspiration for his 1984 horror classic, *A Nightmare on Elm Street*, forever linking the real-life tragedy to one of cinema's most iconic nightmares.

A BIT OF THE OLD ULTRA-VIOLENCE

During World War II, writer Anthony Burgess endured a traumatic event when his wife was assaulted by a group of American soldiers—an experience that later influenced his creation of the controversial novel *A Clockwork Orange*. When the time came to adapt the book for the screen, Burgess initially sold the movie rights to Mick Jagger, who envisioned himself playing the lead role of Alex, with the rest of The Rolling Stones cast as his gang, the Droogs.

However, this version of the film never materialized. Instead, *A Clockwork Orange* was ultimately brought to life by visionary director Stanley Kubrick, with Malcolm McDowell in the iconic lead role. The film became one of the most influential and controversial movies in cinematic history.

From 1973 to 2000, the movie was effectively banned in the U.K.—not due to government censorship, but because Kubrick himself withdrew it from distribution. This decision followed a wave of violent crimes allegedly inspired by the film.

The first major incident occurred in 1973 when a group of men in the U.K. attempted to recreate one of the movie's most disturbing scenes, assaulting a young girl while singing *Singin' in the Rain*, just as Alex does in the film. That same year, a 16-year-old boy brutally beat a younger boy to death while wearing an outfit identical to McDowell's in the movie.

Amid growing public outcry and concern over the film's influence, Kubrick chose to pull it from circulation in the U.K., where it remained unavailable for nearly three decades. Only after his death in 1999 was *A Clockwork Orange* officially re-released, allowing a new generation to experience its dystopian, thought-provoking, and deeply unsettling vision.

THE SHOCKING MAKING OF *THE SHINING*

The Shining premiered on May 23, 1980, as an adaptation of Stephen King's novel, though King himself famously despised the film. His dissatisfaction largely stemmed from director Stanley Kubrick's creative choices, which diverged sharply from King's vision. Kubrick's unique interpretation also influenced casting decisions. At one point, he considered Robin Williams for the role of Jack Torrance—the unhinged protagonist—but ultimately selected Jack Nicholson, believing he naturally exuded a "deranged" presence. Other contenders for the role included Robert De Niro and Harrison Ford.

Despite any casting debates, *The Shining* quickly earned a reputation as one of the scariest films ever made, with tension simmering both on-screen and behind the scenes. Kubrick, infamous for his demanding approach, pushed the production far beyond its initial four-month schedule, stretching from May 1978 to July 1979. His meticulous nature, a hallmark of his work on *Spartacus, 2001: A Space Odyssey,* and *A Clockwork Orange*, made him a legendary yet formidable director, with an obsession for perfection bordering on the tyrannical.

No one felt this intensity more than Shelley Duvall, who portrayed Wendy Torrance. Kubrick's relentless demands took a severe toll on her; she suffered hair loss and frequent illness due to the stress. One particularly grueling scene, in which she frantically ascends a staircase wielding a knife, required 35 takes—akin to climbing the Empire State Building. Other sequences were even more punishing, with one being reshot a staggering 127 times, setting a Guinness World Record.

Kubrick's perfectionism extended to the entire cast, creating an emotionally exhausting atmosphere. Yet, despite the turmoil, *The Shining* cemented itself as a horror masterpiece, solidifying Kubrick's legacy as one of cinema's greatest auteurs.

THE STRANGE ORIGINS OF A WAR EPIC

The Vietnam War, one of the most devastating and controversial conflicts in American history, lasted from 1955 to 1975. While the U.S. officially entered the war in 1965, fighting had already been raging for a decade. The war claimed the lives of over 58,000 American soldiers, while total casualties—including Vietnamese losses—exceeded a million.

The United States' involvement escalated following the Gulf of Tonkin incident on August 2, 1964. The USS Maddox, conducting a covert patrol in North Vietnamese waters, was approached by three torpedo boats. After warning shots were fired, the North Vietnamese retaliated with machine gun fire and torpedoes. While the U.S. ship remained largely unscathed, four Vietnamese soldiers were killed. Though no American casualties occurred, the incident prompted Congress to pass the Gulf of Tonkin Resolution, granting President Lyndon Johnson broad authority to deploy U.S. forces in Vietnam.

More than 3.4 million Americans served in Southeast Asia during the war, with one-third drafted and two-thirds enlisting voluntarily. Among them was Oliver Stone, who specifically requested combat duty. Serving from 1967 to 1968, he was wounded twice and later awarded the Bronze Star and Purple Heart. After returning home, he enrolled at New York University's film school, where he began writing a screenplay based on his wartime experiences, initially titled *Break*.

Stone envisioned The Doors' frontman, Jim Morrison, playing the lead role, with a soundtrack exclusively featuring the band's music.

However, Morrison, plagued by substance abuse, died in Paris in 1971 at the age of 27, leaving Stone's script untouched.

Fifteen years later, Stone's Vietnam film—now titled *Platoon*—was finally made and received widespread acclaim, winning the 1987 Academy Award for Best Picture. Five years later, he directed *The Doors*, a biographical film starring Val Kilmer as Morrison. In a strange twist of fate, the admiral overseeing the Gulf of Tonkin incident that triggered U.S. involvement in Vietnam was none other than George Stephen Morrison—Jim Morrison's father.

SPIELBERG'S LOST FILM

Following the success of *Close Encounters of the Third Kind*, Columbia Pictures eagerly approached director Steven Spielberg for a sequel. However, Spielberg had no interest in continuing the original story. At the same time, he was reluctant to let the studio move forward without his involvement. To retain creative control, he pitched an entirely different idea for a follow-up—a horror-themed film titled *Watch the Skies*.

The concept revolved around a family tormented by malevolent extraterrestrials. Spielberg brought in screenwriter John Sayles—who would later be known for *Eight Men Out*—to develop the script. The aliens in *Watch the Skies* were eerie figures with long, bony fingers that glowed with an unsettling warmth.

Despite its intriguing premise, *Watch the Skies* never made it to production. Spielberg ultimately abandoned the horror-driven approach but salvaged key elements of the story. Instead of terrifying creatures, he envisioned a gentle, endearing alien, transforming the concept into what would become *E.T. the Extra-Terrestrial*—one of the most beloved films of all time.

Though he set aside the sci-fi horror angle, Spielberg didn't discard it entirely. The idea of a family under siege resurfaced in *Poltergeist*, a supernatural horror classic he produced in 1982. In the end, his initial concept for an alien horror film evolved into two iconic movies, further solidifying his legacy as one of Hollywood's most imaginative storytellers.

The Story Behind the Story

LYIN EYES CODY

Iron Eyes Cody was one of Hollywood's most recognizable "Native American" actors, appearing in over 200 films throughout his career, which began in the 1920s. He became a staple in Westerns, often cast as a wise and stoic indigenous figure. Among his notable Hollywood connections was Walt Disney, who featured him in several episodes of *Davy Crockett*.

Despite his extensive film work, Iron Eyes Cody is best remembered for his role in a 1971 Earth Day environmental commercial. In the ad, he watches as careless motorists throw trash out of their car window, polluting the landscape. He solemnly walks over, picks up the litter, and turns toward the camera—his face marked by a single tear rolling down his cheek. This brief yet powerful moment became one of the most iconic public service messages in American history, forever linking Cody to environmental advocacy.

For decades, Cody was celebrated not only as an actor but as a Native American activist, using his platform to advocate for indigenous representation and conservation efforts.

However, his carefully crafted public identity concealed an astonishing truth—Iron Eyes Cody was *not* Native American at all.

Born Espera Oscar de Corti, he was 100% Sicilian-American, with no indigenous ancestry. Despite this revelation, he never broke character, insisting on his fabricated heritage even after journalists exposed his true background. He continued to wear traditional Native clothing, attend indigenous events, and speak on behalf of Native causes, maintaining the persona until his death.

Iron Eyes Cody remains a complex and controversial figure in Hollywood history—an actor whose most enduring role was not on screen, but in real life, as a man who became the identity he portrayed.

THE MONSTER BEHIND THE MOVIE

In 1956, while performing in Birmingham, Alabama, legendary singer Nat King Cole was violently attacked on stage by a group of white men enraged by his integrated audience. The assault was orchestrated by Asa Carter, the leader of a radical Ku Klux Klan splinter group known as the Original Ku Klux Klan of the Confederacy. Frustrated by what he saw as the mainstream Klan's leniency, Carter founded the extremist faction to engage in more aggressive and violent actions.

The following year, Carter's group carried out one of the most horrific hate crimes in Alabama's history. They abducted Judge Edward Aaron, a 34-year-old Black man, brutally assaulted him, and castrated him before leaving him for dead in the trunk of an abandoned car. Six men were arrested for the gruesome attack, but in a shocking act of injustice, their sentences were later commuted by Alabama Governor George Wallace, a staunch segregationist.

Despite his history of racist violence, Asa Carter managed to reinvent himself politically. He became a speechwriter for Wallace, coauthoring the infamous "Segregation Forever" speech. However, after a falling out with Wallace, Carter vanished from the public eye—only to reemerge years later in Florida under a new identity as a novelist. Reinventing himself as Forrest Carter, he wrote *The Rebel Outlaw: Josey Wales*, a novel that was later adapted into the 1976 Clint Eastwood film *The Outlaw Josey Wales*.

Carter's transformation from violent Klansman to bestselling author remains one of the most unsettling reinventions in American history—an example of how even the most notorious figures can manipulate their legacy.

The Story Behind the Story

TRAGIC ORIGINS OF A TELEVISION HIT

In 1955, 14-year-old African American Emmett Till was brutally lynched in Mississippi after Carolyn Bryant Donham, a white woman, falsely accused him of whistling at her in public. The horrific murder shocked the nation, yet the two white men responsible were never held accountable. The injustice deeply resonated with many, including 30-year-old television writer Rod Serling, who sought to address the tragedy through a teleplay.

However, CBS and its sponsors refused to produce a story touching on such a controversial and racially charged subject. Fearful of backlash from white Southern audiences, the network drastically altered Serling's original concept, stripping it of its powerful social commentary. Even references to Coca-Cola were removed from the script to avoid any connection to the South.

Frustrated but undeterred, Serling found another way to explore pressing social issues—through science fiction. He realized that speculative storytelling offered a unique means of addressing complex and uncomfortable topics under the guise of fantasy. By framing real-world injustices within surreal and otherworldly narratives, he could challenge societal norms without direct confrontation.

This creative approach led to the birth of *The Twilight Zone*, a groundbreaking television series that delved into themes of racism, injustice, and human morality. Debuting in 1959, the show became a cultural landmark, using allegory and imagination to illuminate critical social issues while navigating the constraints of censorship and prejudice of its time.

A BROKEN MIND

In the late 1990s, director Ron Howard set out to make a film about a man who battled schizophrenia and achieved remarkable academic success. If you immediately thought of the Academy Award winning film *A Beautiful Mind*, think again. Before directing *A Beautiful Mind*, Howard was originally developing a movie about a man named Michael Laudor, with Brad Pitt attached to star.

Laudor's story initially seemed like the perfect inspirational tale. A Yale graduate from the early 1980s, he began a promising career at a consulting firm before experiencing intense delusions. He became convinced that his room was spontaneously catching fire and that his parents had been murdered and replaced by Nazi spies. As his mental health deteriorated, he left his job but made a remarkable comeback by enrolling in Yale Law School, where he graduated in 1992. With a compelling narrative of resilience and triumph over schizophrenia, Laudor's story appeared destined for the big screen. So why was the film never made?

Just as pre-production was underway, Laudor's condition took a devastating turn. This time, his delusions led him to believe that his pregnant fiancée was not actually his fiancée but an evil alien robot. Acting on this belief, he stabbed her to death. The case shocked the nation, and Laudor was charged with second-degree murder by then-district attorney—and future TV host—Jeanine Pirro. Instead of becoming the subject of an inspiring biopic, he was institutionalized and remains at the Mid-Hudson Forensic Psychiatric Center in New Hampton, New York, to this day.

THE REAL DUNDEEL

Rodney Ansell, born on October 1, 1954, in Queensland, Australia, lived a life defined by survival, adventure, and ultimately, tragedy. At just 15, he moved to the Northern Territory, where he became a skilled buffalo hunter, selling meat to make a living. However, his life took a dramatic turn in May 1977 during what was supposed to be a routine fishing trip in Western Australia. While out on the water, his motorboat capsized—Ansell claimed a whale had caused it—but the real danger lay ahead: he hadn't told anyone where he was going.

Stranded 120 miles from civilization, Ansell salvaged what little equipment he could, including a rifle and knife, and drifted out to sea in a dinghy before finally reaching an island near the Fitzmaurice River. For the next two days, he searched for help, surviving by eating buffalo meat and drinking its blood, all while sleeping in trees to avoid crocodiles. After 50 harrowing days, two Aboriginal men discovered him and guided him to safety. His incredible survival story captured national attention, turning him into an Australian folk hero.

In 1980, a book chronicling his ordeal was published, adding to his growing legend. However, whispers circulated that he hadn't been hunting buffalo at all, but was actually poaching crocodiles. Despite the controversy Ansell began telling his wild story on television programs across Australia, where he caught the attention of actor Paul Hogan. Ansell's rugged persona inspired Paul Hogan to create the character Mick "Crocodile" Dundee. The 1986 film, a global sensation, grossed $328 million.

However, Ansell received neither credit nor compensation for the character, leading him to unsuccessfully sue Hogan. Financial hardship soon followed. Government regulations forced Ansell to cull 3,000 buffalo, straining both his finances and his marriage. His struggles deepened as he spiraled into drug addiction and violent paranoia. In 1999, his descent reached a tragic climax when he fatally shot a police officer during a standoff. A gunfight ensued, and Ansell, just 44 years old, was killed—his extraordinary life ending in the same dramatic fashion in which it had unfolded.

CHAPTER 9

HEORES AND HELLRAISERS

THE MAN WHO DID IT ALL

Christopher Lee, an actor with unparalleled charisma, became an iconic villain in the universes of *Lord of the Rings*, *Star Wars*, *Dracula*, and *James Bond*. Born in 1922 in London, Lee's life was filled with extraordinary moments. As a child, his parents separated, and his mother remarried the uncle of James Bond creator Ian Fleming. It is even alleged that James Bond was based partially on Christopher Lee. As a child, Lee's home was a gathering place for fascinating people, including two Russian men named Felix Yusupov and Dmitri Pavlovich, two of the men who were responsible for the assassination of Russian mystic Grigori Rasputin. This connection would later come full circle when, in 1966, Lee portrayed Rasputin in *Rasputin the Mad Monk*.

Lee's early adulthood years were just as remarkable. In 1939, he witnessed the public execution of Eugen Weidmann in France, the last man to be guillotined. When World War II broke out, Lee enlisted and fought in North Africa and Italy. He survived multiple near-death experiences, including an expedition to climb Mount Vesuvius, which erupted shortly after his ascent. He also worked as a Nazi hunter, capturing and interrogating war criminals.

Lee's acting career began in 1948 with a small role in *Hamlet*, and he went on to star in over 200 films. He became a staple in the horror genre, notably in Hammer's *Dracula* series. His career expanded into the *Star Wars* prequels and *Lord of the Rings*, where he stood out as the evil wizard Saruman. Lee was the only actor in *Lord of the Rings* who had met J.R.R. Tolkien, who had even recommended he play Gandalf (a role taken by Ian McKellen).

Christopher Lee's incredible career continued with collaborations with Tim Burton and even released heavy metal albums before his death in 2015 at age 95. A life filled with action, intrigue, and triumph, Lee's legacy is one for the ages.

THAT WACKY WERNER HERZOG

Werner Herzog, born on September 5, 1942, in Munich, Germany, grew up amid the devastation of World War II. His childhood was defined by extreme poverty—his family often lacked running water, proper shelter, and enough food to survive. At times, they had to share a single piece of bread for an entire day. These hardships forged Herzog's legendary resilience and eccentricity, traits that would later define his career as one of cinema's most uncompromising filmmakers. One such eccentricity was his infamous decision to eat his own boiled shoe after losing a bet with documentarian Errol Morris. Herzog had promised that if Morris completed his film *Gates of Heaven*, he would eat his shoe in front of an audience. Morris finished the film, and true to his word, Herzog cooked and consumed his shoe at the screening.

At 14 years old, Herzog's life took an unexpected turn when Klaus Kinski, a notoriously volatile actor, moved into the same home he shared with his mother. Years later, Kinski would become Herzog's most infamous collaborator, starring in five of his films, including the legendary *Aguirre: The Wrath of God*.

Their professional relationship was chaotic at best. During filming, Kinski once became so enraged by noise on set that he fired a gun at a group of extras, injuring one. Herzog, unfazed, grabbed the gun and threatened Kinski's life if he walked off the film. Kinski stayed, and *Aguirre* was completed.

Their next collaboration, *Fitzcarraldo*, was equally fraught. Filming deep in the Peruvian jungle, Kinski's erratic behavior drove everyone to the edge—including the indigenous extras. At one point, sensing Herzog's frustration, they offered to kill Kinski for him. Herzog declined but later admitted regretting his decision. Their turbulent partnership continued for years, culminating in Herzog secretly plotting to set Kinski's house on fire while he slept. His plan was thwarted when Kinski's dog attacked him before he could carry it out.

Beyond his notorious film productions, Herzog became known for his fearlessness in real life. While promoting *Grizzly Man* in 2005, he was shot with an air rifle during an interview—yet he barely reacted. When asked if he needed medical help, he simply replied, "Why? It was not a significant bullet."

A year later, his calmness under pressure was put to the test again when he rescued a young man from a car crash. After noticing gasoline pooling near the wreckage, Herzog quickly removed the young man from the vehicle, saving his life. That young man happened to be the actor, Joaquin Phoenix. Once the police arrived, he quietly disappeared, never seeking credit for the rescue. The man he saved would go on to star in *Joker* and *Beau is Afraid*, but for Phoenix, the most surreal moment of that night wasn't the crash— it was being saved by Werner Herzog himself.

THE MAN BEHIND THE VOICE

Paul Winchell was born in New York City in 1922 and pursued a uniquely dual career path—attending Columbia Medical School while simultaneously achieving success as a ventriloquist. Throughout the 1950s, he became a television favorite, captivating audiences with his performances. During this time, he met Dr. Henry Heimlich—the same man who would popularize the Heimlich maneuver—and the two began collaborating on a groundbreaking medical innovation: the first artificial heart.

In 1963, nearly two decades before Dr. Robert Jarvik's artificial heart gained widespread recognition, Winchell patented his own version of the life-saving device. His contribution to medical history remains largely overlooked, yet it was a pioneering step in the development of artificial heart technology.

Despite this remarkable achievement, Winchell is best remembered not for his medical invention but for his voice. After securing his place in history with his patent, he transitioned into voice acting, lending his talents to some of the most beloved characters in animation.

He became the unmistakable voice of Tigger in *Winnie the Pooh*, the villainous Gargamel in *The Smurfs*, and the wise Mr. Owl in the classic Tootsie Pop commercial.

Though his name may not be widely recognized today, Paul Winchell's impact—both in medicine and entertainment—continues to resonate, making him one of the most fascinating unsung figures of the 20th century.

HAPPY BIRTHDAY, CHARLIE BRONSON

Charles Buchinsky was born on November 3, 1921, in Ehrenfeld, Pennsylvania, the 11th of 15 children in a working-class Lithuanian immigrant family. After his father passed away when he was just 12, young Charles was forced to work in the coal mines, earning barely a dollar a week. Life was harsh, and he was even known to wear his sister's dress to school—a detail that later added to his tough, no-nonsense persona.

In 1954, to avoid suspicion from the anti-Communist House Un-American Activities Committee, he changed his name to *Charles Bronson*. His breakthrough came in 1960 with *The Magnificent Seven*, followed by *The Great Escape* (1963), solidifying his status as Hollywood's quintessential tough guy. That same year, he appeared in the short-lived series *The Travels of Jaimie McPheeters*, where he earned a reputation for his gruff and intimidating demeanor—though some saw it as the product of a rough childhood rather than genuine hostility.

One day on set, a young child actor gave Bronson a toy rocket for his birthday. Bronson, typically stoic, walked away without a word. Later, that child actor was summoned to Bronson's office, where the hardened actor unexpectedly teared up, confessing it was the first time anyone had given him a birthday present. That child whose gift had affected Bronson so deeply was a young Kurt Russell. Deeply moved, Bronson later returned the gesture by buying Russell a skateboard, and the two were often seen riding around the MGM lot together.

Bronson went on to star in some of the most iconic films of his era, including *The Dirty Dozen* (1967), *Once Upon a Time in the West* (1968), and *Death Wish* (1974), making him one of Hollywood's highest-paid action stars. Though he auditioned for roles like Superman and Snake Plissken in *Escape from New York*, he ultimately lost out to younger actors—including Russell, who would go on to make the latter role his own.

THE ROLE SHE WAS BORN TO PLAY

Actress Teresa Saldana, best known for playing Lenora, the wife of Joe Pesci's character in Martin Scorsese's *Raging Bull*, gained widespread recognition for her performance. However, not all of the attention she received was welcome. In 1982, she became the target of a terrifying obsession that nearly cost her life.

Arthur Richard Jackson, a man who became fixated on Saldana after seeing her in *Raging Bull*, went to disturbing lengths to track her down. He hired a private investigator to locate her mother and, posing as an assistant to Martin Scorsese, tricked her into revealing Teresa's home address. Armed with this information, Jackson traveled to her residence and launched a brutal attack, stabbing her 10 times in broad daylight.

Bystanders intervened just in time, subduing Jackson and saving Saldana's life. Though she suffered severe injuries, she miraculously survived the ordeal.

Two years later, a film version of Saldana's harrowing brush with death titled *Victims for Victims* was released with the role of Teresa Saldana played by none other than Teresa Saldana. By portraying herself, Saldana reclaimed her story, transforming her survival into a powerful statement against stalking and violent crime. Her remarkable bravery not only shaped her legacy as an actress but also made her a vocal advocate for victims' rights, ensuring her ordeal was not forgotten but used to protect others.

SOLO TO THE RESCUE

In 2001, 13-year-old Boy Scout Cody Clawson found himself lost in the vast wilderness of Yellowstone National Park. Alone and disoriented, he relied on his training to survive, eventually seeking shelter in a cave as night fell. With no way of knowing if or when help would arrive, he braced himself for a long, uncertain ordeal.

The next morning, Cody emerged from his makeshift shelter and heard the distant hum of planes overhead. Remembering a crucial survival technique, he used his belt buckle to reflect sunlight, creating a bright glare aimed at the aircraft above. Against all odds, his improvised signal worked, catching the attention of one of the pilots.

To Cody's astonishment, the rescue became even more surreal when the plane landed in a forest clearing and out stepped a familiar figure. As he approached, he was greeted with a simple, "Good morning." The instantly recognizable voice belonged to none other than Harrison Ford.

A devoted *Star Wars* fan, Cody immediately recognized the legendary actor who had famously portrayed Han Solo and Indiana Jones in the *Indiana Jones* series. But this was no Hollywood scene—Ford, an experienced pilot and volunteer for search-and-rescue missions, had quite literally become his real-life hero. In an incredible twist of fate, the boy who idolized Han Solo was saved by him, proving that sometimes, reality can be just as cinematic as the movies.

THE HUMAN SECURITY SYSTEM

Marbella, Spain, is known for its breathtaking beauty, luxurious estates, and peaceful ambiance—qualities that jewelry designer Annette Qviberg had come to love about her home. But in 2009, that tranquility was violently disrupted when three armed burglars broke into her villa, believing it to be filled with money and expensive jewelry.

Inside, they found Annette alone. Overpowering her, they tied her up and threatened her with a knife, demanding to know where she kept her valuables. As they ransacked the villa, one of the burglars stumbled upon a collection of family photos. What he saw made him freeze in place. He quickly signaled for the others to come over, and the three men stared in shock at a picture of Annette standing beside her husband—none other than Dolph Lundgren.

Born in Stockholm in 1957, Lundgren was not only a Hollywood action hero but also a real-life martial arts expert with a master's degree in chemical engineering. Before breaking into acting, he worked as a bodyguard for singer Grace Jones, leading to a romance that eventually brought him to New York.

His big break came in *A View to a Kill* (1985), followed by his legendary turn as Drago in *Rocky IV*. His power was so immense that during filming, he once punched Sylvester Stallone so hard that Stallone ended up in the ICU for nine days.

Back in Marbella, the burglars, realizing whose home they had just invaded, panicked. The mere sight of Lundgren's photo was enough to send them fleeing in terror—despite the fact that he wasn't even home at the time. His reputation alone had turned the would-be robbery into a failed heist, proving that sometimes, fear itself is the best security system.

THE BULLITT BOUNTY

Steve McQueen, legendary star of *The Great Escape* and *Bullitt*, was not just known for his tough-guy roles—he was also a notorious speed demon. His love for fast cars and high-speed races through the streets of Los Angeles became so well-known that the California Highway Patrol once put a bounty on him: a prime rib dinner and a case of scotch for any officer who could successfully pull him over and issue a ticket. However, with his Jaguar far outpacing the patrol cars, McQueen remained an elusive target.

The closest anyone came to catching him was during a high-speed chase when he was pulled over with his pregnant wife in the passenger seat. Thinking quickly, McQueen spun a desperate tale, telling the officer that his wife was in labor and that he needed to get her to the hospital immediately. Sympathetic to the situation, the officer not only let McQueen off the hook but even provided a police escort to the hospital and followed them inside. After a brief wait, the officer left, believing he had helped a distressed couple.

Moments later, McQueen and his wife casually walked out—his wife had never been in labor at all. It was just a well-executed ruse to escape yet another speeding ticket, cementing McQueen's status as the King of Cool.

THE MOST INFLUENTIAL MAN IN SHOW BIZ?

John Milius launched his film career by writing the screenplay for *Jeremiah Johnson* and contributing to *Dirty Harry*. His big break came in 1982 when he directed *Conan the Barbarian*, adapting a script originally written by Oliver Stone to better fit his own vision. Two years later, he helmed the action-packed *Red Dawn*, starring Patrick Swayze and Charlie Sheen.

Beyond directing, Milius penned some of the most iconic lines in movie history. He wrote *Apocalypse Now*'s unforgettable "I love the smell of napalm in the morning," coined "Go ahead, make my day" in *Sudden Impact*, and crafted much of the haunting USS Indianapolis monologue delivered by Robert Shaw in *Jaws*.

However, Milius wasn't just known for his screenwriting—his larger-than-life personality became Hollywood legend. In one infamous meeting about film edits, he casually placed a handgun on the table to emphasize his point, reinforcing his reputation as bold and unpredictable. His eccentricity left such an impression that his friends, the Coen Brothers, based John Goodman's character, Walter Sobchak, in *The Big Lebowski* on him.

Beyond film, Milius also played a role in shaping modern sports. He suggested using an octagon-shaped cage for the UFC, a design that would become a defining feature of mixed martial arts.

With his mix of creativity, audacity, and an unmistakable voice, John Milius carved out a unique legacy in Hollywood—one that continues to influence cinema and beyond.

CHAPTER 10

HORROR AND THE PARANORMAL

THE CURSE OF *THE EXORCIST*

After the massive success of *The French Connection*—which won the Oscar for Best Picture—director William Friedkin was eager to embark on his next project. His choice was an ambitious and chilling one: adapting William Peter Blatty's 1971 horror novel *The Exorcist*.

Released in 1973, *The Exorcist* tells the terrifying story of a young girl, Regan (played by Linda Blair), who becomes possessed by a demonic entity. Her desperate mother (Ellen Burstyn) seeks help from two Catholic priests, portrayed by Max Von Sydow and Jason Miller, to perform a harrowing exorcism. The film became an instant box office phenomenon, ultimately ranking among the highest-grossing films of all time when adjusted for inflation. Its disturbing imagery, shocking special effects, and relentless horror cemented its reputation as one of the scariest films in cinematic history.

However, the production was plagued by eerie incidents that fueled rumors of a *curse*. A fire broke out on set, destroying nearly everything—except Regan's bedroom. Linda Blair suffered a spinal injury during filming, later developing scoliosis.

Several cast members died under mysterious circumstances, including Jack MacGowran, who passed away just a week after completing his scenes, and Vasiliki Maliaros, who died before the film's release. These strange events only added to the film's haunting legacy.

Following *The Exorcist*, Friedkin turned to an equally unsettling subject with his 1980 thriller *Cruising*, a film that remains one of the most controversial of his career. Starring Al Pacino as a cop who goes undercover in New York City's underground gay leather bars to track a serial killer, the movie was inspired by the real-life "bag murders"—a series of gruesome killings in which dismembered bodies were discovered in garbage bags along the Hudson River.

Friedkin's connection to these murders was disturbingly personal. While filming *The Exorcist*, an actor named Paul Bateson—who appeared as a radiology technician in a brief hospital scene—was later revealed to be a real-life killer. In 1977, he was convicted of murdering journalist Addison Verrill, and he later confessed to being involved in the bag murders. This shocking revelation deeply unsettled Friedkin and ultimately influenced his decision to direct *Cruising*, blending fiction with an eerie echo of reality.

From supernatural horror to real-life crime, Friedkin's career remained marked by the unsettling, the unexplainable, and the undeniably disturbing.

THE CURSED CAR

James Dean's passion for acting took root at UCLA, where he studied drama before dropping out to pursue a film career. His breakthrough came in 1953 with *East of Eden*, where his fearless improvisation captivated both audiences and critics. Just two years later, he starred in *Rebel Without a Cause*, a role that cemented his legacy as a Hollywood icon. Tragically, it would be the last film released before his untimely death.

With the fame from *East of Eden* and *Rebel Without a Cause*, Dean indulged in his love for auto racing, purchasing a 1955 Porsche 550 Spyder, which he nicknamed "Little Bastard." He intended to race it in the Salinas Road Race, but Warner Bros. had forbidden him from racing until filming was complete. A week before the event, Dean had an eerie encounter with future Obi-Wan Kenobi actor Alec Guinness, who warned him, "If you get in that car, you'll be dead in a week." The chilling prophecy would come true.

On September 30, 1955, Dean set out for Salinas with his mechanic, Rolf Wütherich, driving along Route 466. At approximately 5:45 PM, a Ford Tudor, driven by 23-year-old Donald Turnupseed, made a sudden left turn onto the highway in front of Dean's speeding Porsche. The two vehicles collided violently. Wütherich was ejected from the car and survived with severe injuries, while Turnupseed escaped with only minor harm. Dean, however, suffered multiple fatal injuries, including a broken neck, and was pronounced dead within an hour at Paso Robles War Memorial Hospital. He was just 24 years old.

In the aftermath, the wrecked Porsche took on an eerie reputation. It was purchased by Dr. William Eschrich, who salvaged its engine for his Lotus IX. During the 1956 Pomona races, Eschrich crashed, though he survived. However, fellow racer Troy McHenry, who had also used parts from Dean's car, was killed when his vehicle struck a tree. The remains of "Little Bastard" were later acquired by George Barris, a custom car builder who planned to restore it. Realizing the car might be unsalvageable, he loaned it to the National Safety Council for a traveling exhibit on reckless driving. At a show in Sacramento, the car reportedly fell from its display, injuring a bystander.

The strange events continued. In 1959, a fire broke out in a garage housing the car, yet the Porsche suffered little damage. Later, a truck transporting the wreck mysteriously crashed, killing the driver.

Then, in 1960, while en route from Miami to Los Angeles, the car vanished without a trace. To this day, its whereabouts remain unknown.

Some speculate that Barris exaggerated or fabricated these incidents to fuel the legend of the so-called "cursed car." Regardless, the myth surrounding "Little Bastard" has only added to James Dean's legacy—a Hollywood star whose life burned brightly but ended far too soon.

THE PHOENIX LIGHTS

On the evening of March 13, 1997, a series of mysterious lights appeared in the skies over Arizona and Nevada. Between 7:30 and 10:30 PM, thousands of witnesses reported seeing the strange formation, sparking widespread speculation about their origin. Among the first to report the phenomenon was an amateur pilot, who was flying into Phoenix, Arizona, with his young son.

As he approached Phoenix Sky Harbor International Airport, the pilot radioed the control tower, describing six large lights arranged in a V-shaped formation. He stated, "I'm going to declare it's unidentified, it's flying, and it's six objects." His report became one of the first officially documented accounts of what is now known as the Phoenix Lights—one of the largest mass UFO sightings in U.S. history.

In the years since, various theories have attempted to explain the lights. The most widely accepted explanation links them to *Operation Snowbird*, a training exercise involving the Air National Guard in Tucson, Arizona.

Five A-10 jets were reportedly flying in formation that night, and their lack of blinking lights, along with their unusual flight pattern, may have caused confusion among onlookers.

However, the explanation hasn't convinced everyone. Ufologists and believers in extraterrestrial activity continue to argue that the lights were something far more extraordinary.

Years later, while watching a television special on the Phoenix Lights, that same pilot suddenly realized the event being discussed was his own report. Turning to his wife, Goldie Hawn, he exclaimed, "That was me! That was me!"—confirming that he, legendary actor Kurt Russell, was the pilot behind one of the most famous UFO sightings in American history.

DAWN BUT NOT FORGOTTEN

When country musician Alex Harvey was just 15 years old, his band won a contest to perform on a local television show in Tennessee. It was a major opportunity, but Alex was apprehensive. Fearing that his mother's struggles with alcohol might cause embarrassment, he asked her not to attend. Respecting his wishes, she stayed away. Tragically, while the show was being filmed, she was involved in a fatal car accident.

The news devastated Alex. Overcome with guilt, he fell into a deep depression, blaming himself for her death. For years, he struggled to move past the pain, convinced that his request had played a role in the tragedy.

Then, one night, as he sat up late writing music, he had an experience that would change his life. As he worked, he noticed a figure sitting in a rocking chair nearby. To his shock, it appeared to be the spirit of his mother. She reassured him that everything was all right, urging him to release his guilt and move forward with his life.

The encounter lifted the heavy weight he had carried for so long. Inspired, Alex poured his emotions into a song—one that would go on to become a country music classic:

"Delta Dawn." The heartfelt ballad later found new life when 13-year-old Tanya Tucker recorded it, turning it into a hit single and cementing its place in music history.

WESTERN HOUSE OF WAX

In 1976, while filming an episode of *The Six Million Dollar Man* at an old west-themed amusement park, the production crew encountered something truly bizarre. The park featured wax figures of infamous outlaws as part of its attractions, adding an authentic touch to the western setting. During preparations for a scene, a crew member attempted to reposition one of the figures, which was posed as if hanging from a noose. As he pulled on the figure, its arm unexpectedly snapped off—revealing a human bone protruding from the severed limb.

What they had assumed was a wax figure was, in reality, a mummified human body. An investigation soon uncovered the shocking truth: the corpse belonged to Elmer McCurdy, a real-life outlaw who had been killed in 1911 after a failed string of robberies ended in a fatal shootout with law enforcement.

Following his death, McCurdy's embalmed body was put on public display and later became part of a traveling carnival exhibit, where it was showcased alongside wax figures of notorious outlaws like Jesse James.

Over the years, his corpse changed hands multiple times, eventually ending up in a wax museum before being used as a prop at The Pike, an amusement park in Long Beach, California.

For decades, McCurdy's body was unknowingly displayed as a curiosity, blending history with legend—until a Hollywood film crew accidentally uncovered the eerie truth.

THE CURSE OF HARRY NILSSON

In 1974, singer-songwriter Harry Nilsson, best known for hits like "Everybody's Talkin" and "Without You," owned a London flat that frequently became a temporary home for musicians passing through the city. That summer, Mama Cass Elliot of The Mamas and the Papas was in London for a residency at The Palladium. Needing a place to stay, she reached out to Nilsson, who readily agreed to let her use his flat.

On July 29, 1974, tragedy struck. Mama Cass went to bed in Nilsson's flat and never woke up. She had suffered a massive heart attack at just 32 years old. Her sudden and shocking death left Nilsson deeply unsettled, and he became wary of allowing others to stay in the apartment, fearing it carried a dark omen.

Fast forward to 1978, when Keith Moon, the legendary drummer of The Who, reached out to Nilsson while back in London. He, too, needed a place to stay. Still haunted by Mama Cass's passing, Nilsson hesitated, fearing that the flat was somehow cursed. But Pete Townshend, Moon's bandmate, reassured him with a dismissive, "Lightning doesn't strike in the same place twice." Convinced, Nilsson reluctantly agreed.

On September 7, 1978, history eerily repeated itself. Keith Moon was found dead in the very same bed where Mama Cass had died four years earlier. He had overdosed on Heminevrin, a drug prescribed to combat alcohol withdrawal. In a chilling coincidence, Moon was also 32 years old at the time of his death.

The tragic pattern surrounding Nilsson's flat cemented its place in rock and roll folklore, forever linked to the premature deaths of two music icons—both taken too soon in the very same room.

SYMPATHY FOR THE DEVIL

Kenneth Anger, born Kenneth Anglemyer on February 3, 1927, in Santa Monica, California, became one of the most influential and controversial figures in independent cinema. A childhood classmate of Shirley Temple, Anger showed an early fascination with the entertainment industry. By the age of ten, he was already making short films, laying the foundation for a career that would challenge artistic and social norms.

As a teenager, Anger developed a deep interest in the occult, particularly the writings of Aleister Crowley, the infamous occultist. This fascination intertwined with his emerging identity as a homosexual, which led to his arrest for "homosexual entrapment" in the 1940s. His defiance of societal norms became a defining characteristic of both his personal life and artistic work.

In 1948, Anger gained notoriety with his short film *Fireworks*, an avant-garde exploration of homosexuality and violence. The film's explicit themes led to another arrest, but it also caught the attention of sex researcher Alfred Kinsey, with whom Anger formed an unusual friendship. Anger even assisted Kinsey in his studies on human sexuality, further blurring the line between his art and personal experiences.

By 1950, Anger had moved to Paris, where he mingled with filmmakers like François Truffaut and Jean-Luc Godard. Encouraged by their interest in Hollywood's dark underbelly, he wrote *Hollywood Babylon*, an explosive, scandal-filled exposé of classic Hollywood's most lurid tales.

Though largely fictionalized, the book became infamous, cementing Anger's reputation as a provocateur.

Returning to the U.S. in the late 1960s, Anger immersed himself in the hippie counterculture and hallucinogenic experimentation. He formed a close bond with Anton LaVey, founder of the Church of Satan, and even became the godfather to LaVey's daughter. This era inspired his most notorious film project, *Lucifer Rising*, an occult-infused cinematic ritual meant to summon the "dark prince." However, the film's production was fraught with chaos—especially when it came to casting the role of Lucifer.

In 1966, Anger invited young men to live with him as part of his unorthodox casting process. One of them was musician Bobby Beausoleil, who contributed to the film's soundtrack before their falling out.

Beausoleil later became entangled with Charles Manson and his cult, eventually committing a murder in what would become the first in a string of Manson Family killings. As these events unfolded, Anger relocated to London, befriending rock stars like Mick Jagger and Keith Richards. The Rolling Stones' "Sympathy for the Devil" was reportedly inspired by Anger's influence.

The troubled production of *Lucifer Rising* took another dramatic turn when Led Zeppelin guitarist Jimmy Page, initially set to compose the film's soundtrack, parted ways with Anger after a bitter dispute. Undeterred, Anger turned to the now-incarcerated Beausoleil, who composed the film's eerie score from prison, further adding to the film's dark mystique.

In the years that followed, Anger continued creating avant-garde films, though less frequently, while maintaining his eccentric persona. His influence remained strong in underground cinema, shaping generations of filmmakers with his boundary-pushing work.

Kenneth Anger passed away on May 11, 2023, at the age of 96. His films, particularly *Lucifer Rising*, continue to leave a lasting imprint on avant-garde cinema, solidifying his legacy as a visionary, an outsider, and a master of the provocative and the surreal.

A HORRIFYING BEGINNING

During the 1960s, as NASA worked tirelessly to land a man on the moon, thousands of engineers contributed to the groundbreaking technology that made it possible. Among them was Ronald Hunkeler, who played a critical role in developing the heat-shielding material that ensured the safe launch and re-entry of Apollo 11. His contributions helped shape one of the greatest achievements in human history.

After a distinguished career at NASA, Hunkeler eventually retired. In 2020, he suffered a massive stroke and passed away. Strangely, just before his death, a priest arrived at his home unannounced to administer last rites. His family was bewildered—no one had called for a priest, and they had no idea how he had found them.

The unexplained visit took on an eerie significance when considering Hunkeler's past. Seventy years earlier, as a young teenager, he exhibited disturbing and violent behavior that terrified his family. Convinced that he was possessed by an evil spirit, they turned to the Catholic Church for help. What followed was a series of intense exorcisms conducted by priests, attempting to drive out the supposed demonic presence.

The case drew attention from local newspapers, but to protect the boy's identity, he was given the pseudonym Roland Doe. Decades later, his chilling ordeal became the inspiration for William Peter Blatty's 1971 novel *The Exorcist*, which was later adapted into one of the most terrifying horror films of all time.

Ronald Hunkeler—a brilliant NASA engineer who helped mankind reach the moon—was also the real-life figure behind one of the most infamous supernatural stories in history. His legacy is an unusual blend of scientific achievement and eerie legend, forever linking him to both the wonders of space exploration and the horrors of *The Exorcist*.

ABOUT THE AUTHOR

CODY TUCKER

A Texas-born storyteller and host of The Cody Tucker Show podcast who has a deep passion for history and pop culture.

A graduate of the University of Texas at Tyler with a bachelor's degree in history, Cody has had a lifelong love for learning and sharing incredible stories from the past. As a viral content creator, his engaging and often humorous takes on historical events and pop culture moments have captivated millions across social media platforms. This is his debut book, bringing his signature voice from the screen to the page.

Printed in Dunstable, United Kingdom